# God Perkins

# God Perkins

## David Pownall

Faber and Faber
3 Queen Square · London

First published in 1977
by Faber and Faber Limited
3 Queen Square London WC1N 3AU
Printed in Great Britain by
The Bowering Press Ltd, Plymouth

ISBN 0 571 10947 0

for Peter Oyston

# one · Summer Lightning

Pilsudski, the artistic director, sat in Weldon Stack's caravan and poured out his troubles much as he would to a confessor. As he explained why he hated Sean Kel, the general manager, so much, Weldon Stack cross-referred every remark to his previous conversation with Sean Kel who had been elucidating his abhorrence of Pilsudski.

"He's the money-man, Weldon, the accountant. Have you ever heard of an accountant choosing plays and auditioning actors? He keeps slipping brown envelopes under my door with bits of advice on how to do the lighting. Life's difficult enough trying to put on shows in this old heap of cast-iron. It's obsolete, like Sean. He's got the idea that he's one of the new actor-managers, raised from the dead. Talk to the bastard for me, make him stick to his own side of the business. I'll plant him before long and break his nose again."

Pilsudski was talking about the accident which had happened during the previous season while the mechanized theatre was established in Accrington. One evening Sean had been at the foyer entrance in his evening suit welcoming a block-booking of Rotarians when a gust of wind had blown the photographic display cabinet off the side-panels and fractured the general manager's long Gaelic neb. Pilsudski had laughed for a fortnight while Sean was out of commission, plotting in the Infirmary.

"Look at this. Read it for yourself. Now the Irish moron is a psychiatrist . . ."

Weldon Stack took the brown envelope. As he read it he nodded so his huge afro bush of hair bobbed.

MEMO

THE GENERAL MANAGER to THE ARTISTIC DIRECTOR
*Subject: The Unfathomable Grass.*
It has come to my notice that the walk-out rate from Ben McHugh's play is now up to 65.7% per performance, leaving 33.3% as the paying residue as the people who leave usually demand their money back. It is my opinion that a profound moral affront is caused by the scene in Act 1 where the defective violence-obsessed second lead uses the WRAC Lieutenant's pectoral regions as a billiard-table. I recommend that the scene is re-written to prevent delicate sexual sensibilities be-

ing wrecked for life. Our mental hospitals are full enough.

*Sgd* Sean Kel

"See what I mean, Weldon? He doesn't live in the same world as me. That's one of the best scenes in the play. Brings the house down. What am I going to do about him?"

Both the artistic director and the general manager were anxious to enlist Weldon Stack's support because the front-of-house manager was reputed to be the most cunning manipulator of internal politics in the organization. He could arrange a *détente* at a moment's notice, or get a series of head-on collisions under way which would reduce the Dramacart Moving Theatre Company to emotional rubble in half-an-hour. Weldon Stack, with his strange slavonic eyes and crooked smile, had the mind of a Great World War foreign minister.

"Sean is a megalomaniac."

Weldon Stack rubbed his long thin nose and poured out another two glasses of red wine.

"Hmmm?"

"He's mismanaged the theatre."

"Ah."

"He's a nepotist."

Weldon Stack sipped his wine and emptied a small tin of Japanese smoked oysters on to a slice of split wheat bread.

"Sean has no *relatives* working for the company."

"All right, but it's the same thing. Glenda was the box-office girl until Sean started screwing her. Then he said he'd found hidden talents for administration in the cow and persuaded the board to make her assistant manager. It's laughable."

"But a *fait accompli*," Weldon Stack smiled foxily, spreading the tiny orange oysters over the brown bread with a carmine and grey fish-slice. "You should have objected at the time."

"I had too much on my mind."

There was a pause as the front-of-house manager bit into his hors-d'œuvre.

"Would you do me a favour and turn that rotisserie for a moment? The mechanism isn't working. I don't want that grouse overdone."

Pilsudski took the tiny aluminium handle and turned it so

the purple carcass rotated over the infra-red grill in Weldon Stack's portable *Cordon Bleu* Gastronome Kit. He felt slightly ill at ease in such a pose, remembering Lambert Simnel in the kitchen of Henry Tudor. The only difference between the historical scene and that being played in the front-of-house manager's caravan was that Weldon Stack was ten times the crafty diplomat that Henry Tudor had ever been.

"Glenda's mother is on the county council. She is the aunt of Rhoda Pearson who is the children's theatre adviser to the Theatrefund. Glenda's father is a magistrate in Icklington. Last year he quashed fourteen parking charges for us when we broke down in the High Street coming north. Also Glenda has a godfather who is the brother of the owner of our site in Mexport. She could get us thrown off any time. You see Peter, Glenda has *power*, and Glenda has money. That's an unbeatable combination. I think Sean started screwing her to reinforce his own position. With Glenda behind him, he's a difficult man to oust. You know she doesn't have to work for Dramacart. She chose it as her project, her pet charity. She bestowed herself on us. Sean accepted, on our behalf."

Pilsudski's mouth was drawn down at the corners. Sadly he continued turning the little aluminium handle, his mind elsewhere, toiling through the future and how to bundle Sean and his heavyweight girlfriend out of their seats of power.

"Stack, old son, you know who the next general manager will be if we get rid of Sean? I can fix it. And next year when we get a *proper* theatre, you know who will be the general manager of that? From there? The whole theatre industry is open to you. One day you'll be the GM at the National, or the Sydney Opera House. Oh I keep up my Australian connections, sport. Do you get my meaning?"

Weldon Stack nodded his high bank of hair and put a hand over Pilsudski's as it wound the rotisserie.

"I think it's done now. Just prick the breast with that fork and put that small saucepan on the hot-plate will you?"

Pilsudski stood up and started waving his arms about.

"Christ, Stack, you've got to commit yourself! I'm offering you a great deal."

Weldon Stack slipped the rod out of the grouse and stirred his garlic and cream sauce with a green Biro, his slanted eyes watchful as the artistic director flailed his fists in the air.

"Stack, we'll have the best theatre in the country. They'll

3

be queueing ten deep to get in. The best actors, the best material. We'll get Ben to write some new stuff, transfer it to the West End and make a bomb. Not for ourselves, but for the new theatre. People will come from Russia and America to see how it should be done. And you'll be running it with me! Now, we must get shut of Sean! Help me!"

Weldon Stack carved the grouse with a razor-blade held in a handkerchief. As the slivers fell from the breast he dipped them in the saucepan and put the flesh into his mouth.

"Mmmm, delicious. Peter, what you have to do is make a success of the season. We need a success, a breakthrough. Be daring, pursue the unorthodox course. Why not do a musical? All right, I know you're tone-deaf, but you can get help. Better than just *a* musical, why not a *new* musical. Dig up some character who needs revaluation and is intrinsically entertaining. You could do worse than St Paul. There's a queer fish if you like. My brother might be prepared to do the music. I can get him over from Canada in a week. You'd mesh with Jules, strike sparks. He'd do it for love."

"Stack, that's not Ben's style. He's interested in the profound issues like Death, Time, Love. He's not sold on trivia."

"You're the first person I've heard who's called St Paul trivial. You could have a terrific scene where he falls off his horse on the road to Damascus . . ."

Weldon Stack knew that he had hit the right note. He could see it in the artistic director's face. An eerie light glowed in his green eyes and his broad mouth hung open.

"You mean we could have a horse on-stage?"

"Why not?" Weldon Stack mumbled through a mouthful of grouse. "We had a guillemot in *The Seagull*."

"But that was dead. I'd want a *live* horse."

"You know how Bert feels about having children and animals in shows."

Pilsudski dismissed Bert, the stage-manager, with a flurry of his arms.

"He'll do as he's told. If I want St Paul falling off a live horse, that's how it will be. We can put ramps up the side of the trailer and have a stall. It'll be easy. I'll see Ben tonight."

Weldon Stack reached under his bunk and brought out a *poire belle helene* in a jam-jar. As Pilsudski, chin in hand, lank hair hooding his fiercely shining eyes, left the caravan to work out the details of the new production, the front-of-house manager dug into his sweet with a plastic banker's card and smiled with two sorts of relish.

## two · A few verses of Ben McHugh's poetry which he read aloud to Joan Earth in a derelict slate-quarry under a full moon, and some ensuing dialogue

MCHUGH *From this peeling boudoir*
*the precise crystallography*
*of summer stars is made plain,*
*the blazed design spells out*
*a lust as hopeless as post-coital*
*sadness . . .*

JOAN EARTH That says it all Ben.

MCHUGH Is that rusty hawser hurting your back?

JOAN EARTH I shaved my legs for you, Ben.

MCHUGH Look around you.

JOAN EARTH Ben, it's so *craggy*, so downright masculine.

MCHUGH A desert. Holes in the ground. A broken-down industry. Where are the quarrymen now? What have they left us but their off-cuts and throw-aways? We are a generation of scavengers.

JOAN EARTH Was that your poetry, Ben, or were you just talking?

MCHUGH I was just talking, though I might just write it down. Hold on. Pass my trousers. You inspire me Joan. Christ, I adore your mouth. What a mouth.

JOAN EARTH Huh-huh

MCHUGH Have you got a Biro?

JOAN EARTH Where would I have a Biro?

MCHUGH Listen to this.

JOAN EARTH I wish I could write poetry.

MCHUGH Don't wish that on yourself.

JOAN EARTH Can we get off this concrete donkey-engine mounting and find somewhere more comfortable?

MCHUGH I wanted you to be a sacrifice to the dark gods of the Industrial Revolution.

JOAN EARTH Why don't I think of things like that?

MCHUGH Because you just *are*, Joan, you exist completely within yourself. You are honest and innocent. I am the fool for asking questions. I wish I were you. I want to be a living part of you.

JOAN EARTH Ben, I'm not all that honest. Not really.

MCHUGH This is a poem I wrote about the Lancaster–Preston canal.

JOAN EARTH Great!

MCHUGH Bridge number ninety-four. You know all the bridges are numbered by the British Waterways Board?

JOAN EARTH Great!

MCHUGH *There is nothing here*
*my absence would not cure:*
*without me musing on this path*
*the land might breathe tranquillity*
*and sense,*
*filter the journey's gold*
*from this canal, construct*
*a morning from plain innocence* . . . (slow fade)


three · Nocturne

Joan Earth had chosen her stage-name with care. When her letters arrived on the desks of theatre directors, television and film-casting executives and unscrupulous flesh agents, that name struck them a blow which was synchronized to fall with the effect of her dark slumberous eyes gazing from her photograph. Backed up by the reproduction of a deep and devastating cleavage twelve inches below her half-open mouth, no human being past puberty could simply throw Joan Earth aside. Under that cascade of black curls brooded an unforgettable face. Even her nose was a shaft of pure erotic architecture. But no pix could do justice to her body. What was revealed in the head and shoulders was designed to lead any stranger to dream of what lay beyond. Joan had thought of having a small plastic 45 rpm record of her voice to send out with her job-hunting brochure, but an early taping experiment had demonstrated that her profound vibrations were beyond the powers of the miserable, inanimate equipment. There was just not enough throb in the machine.

6

To catch up with Joan needed the gift of life, and desire, and sexual courage. All of these were in the blood of McHugh as he drove his battered sports car down the rough quarry road, the silencer trailing and striking sparks off the rocks. From his exhaust came a virile roar which blended exactly with his mood. Sheep reared up from behind stone walls and scampered away up the fells, roosting birds rose to a moonlit dawn. Farmhouse windows suddenly became blocks of gold as hard-worked men groped in cupboards for shotguns and sleepy fingers wrestled with bolts on dog kennels. But McHugh was too quick for them, his headlamps destroying the dark along the winding road as he drove with the tranquil fire of Joan's urgent physical responses burning in his memory. She stimulated, liberated his struggling brain.

Together, forehead to forehead, they shot beneath the robot barrier to the Borrans Field car-park site and drew up behind the rear caravans. In sheer exuberance McHugh stamped on the accelerator and raised the engine to a final bellow. Beryl turned to Joe Woodhead who was sleeping off her revenge and asked him to leave. Sean switched on his bedside light and made a note of the time of the audial assault and tried to estimate its decibel intensity, and Lulu drank the last of her Nescafé and peeped through the window to see if McHugh was going to Joan Earth's caravan for the rest of the night or was going back to his own to face Beryl, now radiant with her revenge. Bert and Fred (the engineer) lay in their oily cots covered with oily blankets and cursed all fookin intellectuals while the actors and actresses grimly noted yet another breach of the understanding whereby everyone had to think of others when on tour with such a small, tight-knit company, and planned to complain to the artistic director in the morning.

As Joe Woodhead climbed out of the rear window of the caravan McHugh was waiting for him with Joan Earth.

"What kind of mood is she in?" McHugh asked in a low voice.

Joe Woodhead stalled, then muttered uneasily as he slid his back leg out of the aperture: "Are you talking to me?"

"Come on, Joe, speak up. Is it worth me going in or should I stay with Joan? What do you think?"

"That's none of my business."

"Yes, it is, Joe. You're one of the family."

"Don't try and be funny with me McHugh."

"All I'm asking you to do is save me some trouble. You know I'm scared of Beryl."

Joe Woodhead looked at Joan Earth who was only a shape in the moon-shadows. He felt split right down the middle. With a surly grunt he started to move away past McHugh but was caught by Pilsudski who appeared from behind the Green Room trailer with a sheaf of papers.

"Don't go, Joe. I want you to hear this. We've got it, Ben! Got it! You're going to break through with this. When you've written this new play about St Paul you'll be made man, no looking back, nothing but success after success, Christ it turns me over just thinking about it . . ."

"What d'you mean, I'm *going* to write?" McHugh protested. "I decide that . . . don't I?"

"We're going to have a talking horse!" Pilsudski screeched with enthusiasm. "Think of it Ben. How many writers get a chance to write dialogue for a talking horse?"

"A horse? In the Dramacart? We've only got a fly-height of eleven feet. What happens if the horse rears? It would go through the roof."

"It won't rear. We'll get a trained animal. It will be as obedient as an actor," Pilsudski chattered, waving his papers around. "Christ, Ben, I can't wait to see the script. When can I have it? Next Monday?"

Joe Woodhead saw the avenging outline of Beryl framed in the rear window of the caravan and sidled away, mounting the steps of the chemical-toilet vehicle.

"Can you wait until this is over before you go in there?" Lulu requested from her vantage-point under the axle. "It's that drumming noise I can't stand."

Joe Woodhead sighed and turned away towards a silvered bank of bramble bushes and privacy.

"As far as I can remember the story of St Paul, the horse *has* to rear up when the blinding light hits him on the road to Damascus. St Paul can't just fall off like a dead weight with no impetus from the animal. We must have a real rear from the horse otherwise it will look artificial."

"Will you come to bed and shut up?" Beryl said menacingly from the rear window. "I know you're trying to drive me out of my mind, you sod."

McHugh gave his wife a crinkly, begging smile.

8

"Won't be a minute, love."

"Now!" Beryl hissed with steel in her voice. "God, you make me sick."

"Ben, leave the technicalities to me. The horse is no problem, honest. I've done shows with white whales, goats, anything you can think of. Christ man I can remember in Melbourne once we did a late-night show with a dozen wallabies playing cricket with the head of an aborigine sub-chieftain. So leave it to me Mr Writer. Just you exercise the old inner creative forces and we're laughing."

Pilsudski hugged his papers to his orange union shirt and shook his head with thoughtful zest. Dreams were building up in his brain like cumulus clouds on an open horizon.

Beryl switched off the light in the caravan and got into bed. From where she was lying she had a clear view of McHugh's head silhouetted against the full moon. In her right hand she weighed a glass cube bottle of night-cream. If one of the sharp corners hit him in the pressure-points around his throat and skull, it could kill him. Then Beryl would be free. She could get out of this poky caravan, find a good school to teach in, get married to one of the bachelors in the staff-room and settle down on the quietest private housing-estate she could find. There would be a deep-freeze and a colour television, an ironing-board which came out of a cupboard on a hinge, a two-chime doorbell with golden pipes and peace.

As Beryl threw the glass cube, Pilsudski became so excited with the prospect of the new musical play about St Paul and the success it would bring, that he threw his helicoptering arms around McHugh's neck and hugged him. The night-cream flashed past the intended victim and landed in the ditch which was flanked by the bramble bushes where Joe Woodhead was having a piss. Joe Woodhead thought that Beryl had thrown the glass cube at him in revenge for their revenge, about which she sometimes felt guilty. With a low cry of unintelligible despair the aspiring actor fell to his knees and wished to holy God that he was back at home with his mother in Ilford.

As soon as Sean heard what Pilsudski was planning, he called in Weldon Stack. The play that the artistic director was pulling out of the repertoire was *A Midsummer Night's*

9

*Dream* and it was not only Sean's favourite—he had played The Wall in the Belfast Boys' Brigade production in 1953—but it was drawing the best audiences of the four plays at present in rotation. Now the artistic director had gone too far. He was cutting his own throat to further the interests of McHugh. Not only that, but Sean had been planning to ship the whole production of *A Midsummer Night's Dream* over the lake to put on a special performance for a millionaire friend of Glenda's from Birmingham who had a large eighteenth-century house on an island. There was going to be a party for the leading lights in Orrestwater society and the play would be the centre-piece of the evening. Sean did not intend to charge Glenda's friend Ed for the performance. It would be a cultural gift to people who could appreciate it, and the setting on the lawns of the house which swept down to the still, brooding lake, would be perfect. Shakespeare himself would have approved.

"Weldon, how am I going to stop him?" Sean moaned.

"Ah-ha!"

"Should I go down to the Theatrefund and put my case?"

"That depends."

"Depends on what?"

"What McHugh comes up with. He's started writing. Pilsudski and McHugh didn't go to bed last night. They've already instructed Bert to go out and find a docile horse that can do a controlled rear. It's all settled as far as they're concerned. The show is scheduled to open in two weeks. I've ordered the tickets and posters. The show's called *The Blinding Light*. My brother's flying over from Ottawa to do the music. I sent him a telegram this morning."

Sean stared in disbelief at his front-of-house manager.

"Which side are you on, Weldon?"

"The side which wins, Sean."

"It can't work! The audiences up here aren't interested in that kind of trendy rubbish. They like the classics, serious drama, north-country comedies. You know what they're like. Weldon, talk to Pilsudski. Get him to cancel it, or at least postpone it until I can call a board-meeting."

Weldon Stack shook his head. He explained to the general manager that it was impossible to stop Pilsudski once he got an idea in his head and decided to bring it to life. *The Blinding Light* was as good as on-stage already. Nothing could stop the whirling-dervish Australian, nor the steady tapping of McHugh's travel-riter.

"And don't forget, Sean, it might be good."

"And if it isn't?"

"Then we'll have to cut our losses and get rid of Pilsudski and McHugh."

"You'd help me do that?"

"Of course. They'd be jeopardizing my position. If the season is a failure someone perverse enough will think of blaming the front-of-house manager."

Weldon Stack left the general manager's caravan. Sean watched him crossing the clear ground in the middle of the ring of vehicles. There was an indeterminate confidence in his gait and the bobbing of his frizzy hair. Weldon Stack was going places. He was a professional down to the heels of his fashionable zip-up boots and the striped night-shirt which he wore tucked into his bell-bottomed maroon corduroys. The exterior was that of a colourful drop-out, a bohemian non-participant in the rat-race: the interior would have been perfectly at home on the board of a stockbroking business which dealt exclusively with asset-strippers.

"You'll have to watch Weldon," Glenda said firmly. "He's too ambitious."

"It will take more than Weldon to outwit me," Sean muttered determinedly. "I've been running this place too long to be taken in by an in-out merchant like him. When Weldon is on the dole, the Dramacart will still be doing its job, taking theatre to the rural areas, and I'll be with it. We'll win in the end, won't we?"

Glenda clutched Sean's head to her Shetland jumper with the old Nordic designs and genuine pewter clasps. Gently her fingers sought the craggy brow of her lover. She did not reply to his question. Her mind was buckled to the problem of finding out from Sean what exactly she was expected to *do* as his assistant manager. Perhaps in these bumps and furrows was the answer. To be with her love in his worries, to share the burden. Together they would keep the old war-surplus turtle groaning through the valleys and puffing up the mountains, bringing theatre to the theatre-less areas. It was a life's work.

"Sean."

"Yes?"

"Couldn't we be co-general manager?"

"Eh?"

"We could get married and share everything. Our lives could be one. Work and leisure would be unseparated. We would have wholeness. Don't you think wholeness is so important? It's everything."

Sean registered Glenda's claim in the back of his mind. He would have to accede, he knew that. It would make no real difference to their relationship though. They were completely compatible. That was not the issue of the day. What mattered was the strategy for out-manœuvring Pilsudski. Sean had two choices. Either he could use this present idiocy of Pilsudski's to bring him before the board and to state quite plainly and irrevocably that it was now a case of either Pilsudski resigned or Sean would; or to wait and see what happened with *The Blinding Light*, making it clear to both the Theatrefund and the board that the general manager had been bulldozed into accepting the new venture without ever being consulted as to his views on the viability of the enterprise. He could approach Pilsudski about the special performance on Ed's island as a separate matter. Even the Dramacart actors might be able to remember their lines for seven days after the play was removed from the repertoire.

Sean outlined these choices to Glenda over a breakfast of Alpen, Cumberland sausage and Mocha coffee pre-ground from the Orrestwater high-class grocery and provisions store run by Glenda's Aunty Rebecca.

"Well, co-general manager, what do you think we should do?"

Glenda lowered her heaped spoonful of Alpen, raisins and cereal flakes spilling on to her tweed-slung lap as her hand shook with pure joy.

"Oh Sean, we're going to be completely together? We're going to be one soul, with one goal?"

Sean smiled carefully, adjusting his rugged eyebrows so as not to convey an impression of surrender or gross emotionalism.

"Unity is what we need on the business side now. This is crisis-time. We must save the Dramacart from Pilsudski and McHugh. With you by my side I could take on the world."

Glenda dashed her spoon back into the plate and leaned

across to fold her man in her arms, tears streaming down her plump cheeks. Only a few months ago she had been a nobody, a very slow typist, a puller of weeds in her mother's English country garden, an attender of auctions and fêtes, a rosy church-going country girl with a hopeless quest in her heart. Theatre was her dream-life. She could not dance. She could not sing. She could not act. But she could bustle. With an iron-hard deliberation she planted a kiss on Sean's forehead.

"You won't regret this, love. How much do I get?"

"Two thousand two hundred."

"How much do you get?"

Sean paused and appeared discomforted.

"Two thousand five hundred."

"I must get the same as you. That's essential. Nothing must separate us. We must be together. Five thousand a year isn't bad is it? When will you talk to the board? I'll do a letter for you. What time's the post?"

"Glenda darling, you know how I agree with you about sharing our life's work in every way, but I don't think the board will accept the principle of you getting the same salary as me for a while. I have been doing this job for five years and it is only my annual increments that have boosted me up to two thousand five hundred . . ."

Glenda sat down and resumed her breakfast. She kept her eyes on her plate and did not speak again for an hour. Sean tried to read the newspaper, put it down, started on some box-office returns, did the washing-up, put the breakfast things away, walked round the caravan, checked the calor-gas bottle, looked at the sky. When he re-entered the caravan Glenda was still sitting in her chair, not talking, her eyes on the floor. Sean stood behind her and stole an arm under her armpit to a large soft breast.

"My love . . ."

Glenda wrenched his hand away and shot to her feet, catching the general manager in the face with her head. He stumbled away and sat down on the bunk, eyes streaming. Glenda turned on him, blonded hair floating.

"Look Sean, no more pushy-pushy for you until you promise that I'll get the same as you. It's not fair otherwise. How can we possibly live together in this kind of atmosphere of jealousy?"

Sean nodded. After Glenda had typed out the letter to the chairman of the board, Sean walked into town and posted it, then walked up the High Street to the jewellers to choose an engagement ring. Not that any choice was necessary. Glenda had specified the size, type and price of finger-ornament that was appropriate for a co-general manager of a mobile theatre. It had to have that gipsy flair, a touch of extravagance, maybe a flamboyance in the size of the diamond, oh Sean knew what she meant! He could see into the heart of all her dreams. When he returned he hid the ring in a locked drawer in the box-office and went into conference with Glenda on the problem of *The Blinding Light*.

## four · Generators

Old Fred, the engineer of the Dramacart, fingered his oily collar as he stood up in the company meeting which had been called to hear complaints about the resident writer's Midget. Fred did not enjoy being in the auditorium when he made his speech, even though his friend Bert was by his side rolling cigarettes for him. What Fred would have preferred would have been a front-stage spotlight and some music as a background. As a marine engineer in the Merchant Navy he had sailed several times round the world and seen every kind of stage-show you could name. From Cairo to Tokyo, from Hamburg to San Francisco, Fred had been there, carefully observing the artistes. There was nothing these kids could teach Fred about acting. Given the chance he would have joined the cast, done any small part, just to prove his point. Sean had been deaf to his entreaties, as had Pilsudski. So the company meetings were the only opportunity which Fred had to display his unique gift of verbal communication.

"Even when I was gun-running from Tunis up the Aegean to Marseilles, we considered each other. When you went off watch at night you didn't have to put up with this kind of thing. If we'd been caught it would have been the firing-squad for all of us."

"Fookin inconsiderate I call it," Bert muttered as he licked along the cigarette paper for his friend. "No sense of fookin goodwill towards men."

14

"In the subs when we were shadowing German battleships in the Atlantic you could rely on the crew to give you a fair deal. When a feller got his head down, that was it. It could be his last night on earth with the water pouring through the holes from the depth-charges. Today people don't consider other people. They just do as they like."

"Fookin intellectuals," Bert grumbled. "Think they own the place. Getting me out first thing in the morning looking for well-behaved fookin horses."

"It's not on. It's inhuman. Where's the old spirit of comradeship? Look at the bags under my eyes."

Fred poked an oily finger at his oily eye and adjusted his dentures with a flick of his tongue. Then he sat down and lit the buckled cigarette that Bert pressed into his hand.

"Fookin brilliant," Bert whispered, holding out a lighted match. "He's impressed, the Aussie bastard. See the way he's looking at you?"

Pilsudski was staring at Fred as though seeing him in a new light. Fred half rose to his feet, anticipating the production of a contract from the artistic director's jacket pocket.

"Fred, I think Ben McHugh has got the message, haven't you, Ben?"

McHugh nodded vigorously from row D where he was tapping away at a portable typewriter held on his knees.

"I don't think there's any doubt about the way the whole company feels on this point," the Equity deputy chipped in. "We can't be expected to give of our best if we aren't rested. The body can only take so much without sleep. Then it starts to crack up."

A murmur of agreement passed along the row of actors and actresses who had all been to see Pilsudski that morning complaining of headaches, nausea, nervous breakdowns, bee-stings, jaundice and acute diarrhoea. During the movement class Murphy Winspear had not been able to get up after adopting the lotus position and Fiona McPhee had been sick over the lighting-board, receiving an electric shock straight through her larynx.

"What I was thinking, Fred, was that you could give us a hand. You know we're in the middle of a period of really hard work, trying to get this new play of Ben's on stage . . ."

Fred passed a nervous oily hand through his oily hair. This was it. His chance. Pilsudski had seen the light. Fred started to clamber over the seats in front, his oily overalls marking the red plush.

"I thought you could repair Ben's silencer for him. He can't take time off from writing the script at the moment you see. Could you do that for us?"

Fred paused, one leg in row C, the other in row B.

"You're joking."

"Christ, Fred, you are an engineer aren't you? What's a silencer to an expert like you?"

"Let him fix his own car."

"He can't, Fred. He's got no money and no time. We have to do it for him."

His long face darkened with disappointment, Fred sat down. When would Pilsudski see what was staring him in the face? Why give the mature roles to kids straight out of drama school when there was a man of forty-nine already in the company, bursting with the will to get up there and give his all? For a moment Fred thought about the future. There would be other plays, other times. His luck might change. Pilsudski might get the bullet. If Sean took over the artistic side then Fred would certainly stand a better chance. Sean believed in the well-tried values of working men. He thought theatre belonged to ordinary people, not these nervy poofs, drunks and layabouts. Fred had heard on the grapevine that the Dramacart was in the throes of a power-struggle. All he had to do was bide his time and hope. He agreed to mend the silencer while under his breath he joined Bert's hushed croak of "fookin intellectual" as a subsidiary curse.

"But he can help me get the Perkins off the back of the Scammel in return. He's big enough. I can't manage that by myself," Fred added savagely. "Don't foget that I need help sometimes."

"What's the Perkins?" Pilsudski asked.

"The generator."

"What are you taking the generator off for?"

"Glenda got some extra maintenance grant for the lorries. We're using it to buy a new generator. It's arrived. The old one is on its last legs. That's why the lights have kept failing."

"So we've got *two* generators now?"

"That's right," Fred said tiredly, "a new one and an old one."

Pilsudski clapped his hands and marched up and down the stage.

"Fred, you're a genius. Hear that, Ben? Two generators. We've got a spare generator. Well done, Fred! It's a godsend. It's just what we need."

There was a long dumbfounded silence as Fred tried to work out what he had achieved by fiddling his budget in order to get a new generator so he could sell the old one to a friend in Workington who was opening a poultry-farm in an outlying district. He looked shifty and uncomfortable, wishing that he had never raised the question of McHugh giving him a hand to get the old generator off its mountings.

"Ben, stop typing for a minute. Fred's given me a brilliant idea. We can have the old generator on stage in the new show."

McHugh put his travel-riter on the floor and informed the artistic director that he would not accept orders to include ancient machinery in his script.

"Ben, think of the symbolic value! What is a horse? A symbol of creative power. What is a Perkins? Its modern counterpart! We can span the centuries, concertina time. With the generator and the horse we can suggest complete universality of theme."

The Equity deputy raised the question of noise.

"Fred can fit a silencer on it, like he's going to do on Ben's car."

"Peter," Vivienne Brasenose spoke in a sharp, precise manner as she stood up. "We think that it's going to be hell enough with a horse on stage with us, never mind Fred's dreadful old generator which is always breaking down. We can't mend the damn thing."

"You won't need to. Fred will mend it if it breaks down."

"I'll have to be on stage to do that," Fred retorted, quick as a flash.

The Equity deputy winced.

"Fred love, that would be rather a problem."

"Look mate, I'll be all right up there. I know all the ropes. I won't let you down. Can I have my name in the programme?"

"Ben, it's got to go in. *The Blinding Light*, where else would it come from? The generator can be a symbol of the creative power of God."

"I could be God!" Fred shouted as he clambered over rows B and A and jumped on to the stage. "I'll be there, keeping it all working."

McHugh groaned and pressed his brow against the back of the seat in front. Much as he liked and admired Pilsudski, there were times when he wished to be left alone with his Muse. He racked his brain, trying to accommodate the Perkins in his plot.

"Couldn't Fred hide behind it disguised as something? Does he have to be visible?"

"Of course I've got to be visible!" Fred cackled as he tested the boards around centre-stage for strength. "What's the point of having God in the programme if you can't see Him?"

"All I can think of is . . ." McHugh scratched his curly hair, forcing his mind into gigantic leaps and bounds, "if we make the generator into a mechanical horse, a replica of the live horse, we can get a *doppelgänger* effect . . ."

"Christ, man, I've got one of those in my tool-box!" Fred yelled triumphantly. "You're on!"

McHugh knocked on Weldon Stack's caravan door and begged some lunch off him. Beryl had locked herself in and was writing a list of all the available bachelors in the staff-room of the remedial school where she was supply-teaching. The moment of truth had arrived. Starting from Monday she would be building a new life for herself, devoid of revenge and suffering. When McHugh had demanded food to keep him going during the creative process, Beryl had told him that unless he left her alone she would take the rubber pipe from the calor-gas cylinder, put her head in a plastic bag, hold the pipe under her nostrils, turn on the tap and breathe deeply. McHugh had wandered away, his mind locked on the problem of imagining a conversation between a Perkins generator ridden by oily old Fred as God, and a docile horse with a controlled rear ridden by Joe Woodhead who had been cast as St Paul because he had a face that was vaguely like Charlton Heston's.

"Stack, why does Peter think he can tell me to write to order? Can't you talk to him? I know he's a great director and I'm a Pilsudski fan, but he doesn't understand what a writer has to go through before he can actually re-create

18

reality into his own form and fill space which was previously empty with a new and original shape in terms of action, images and human relations . . ."

"Write some good songs for my brother. He likes sad subjects but I've heard him do some light stuff that wasn't bad. A bit like Offenbach. Do you like Offenbach?"

"Do you think the show is feasible? In the time we've got? I don't want a flop on my hands." McHugh sighed as he spread Canadian caviare on Ryvita.

The engineer poked his head through the door.

"If you give me a few lines, say ten or twenty, I'll let you in on my Cunard Line pension for twelve months, two quid a week . . ." he chattered, his long tongue rattling his dentures. "Anything you want Ben, just name it."

"Fred," McHugh said patiently, "we haven't even squared this with Equity. We may be able to get permission for you to be on stage without being paid, but not if you've got lines to say."

"That's no problem. Sean can pay me, then I'll give you the money. I don't want the money, I want the lines."

Weldon Stack beckoned the oily engineer into the caravan but did not ask him to sit on his Moroccan tribesman's blanket. Instead he pointed to a box that was painted scorched earth and carried a brass Spanish jug with tall dried grasses in it, tastefully mingled with marigolds.

"Have a seat, Fred. Here."

Weldon moved the jug and confronted the stage-struck engineer.

"Fred, there are certain things you must understand. The acting profession is overcrowded. At any one time seventy per cent of its members are out of work," he began, his afro hair nodding sagely. "You can't just walk into it. There are agreements with unions to think of . . ."

"Look Weldon, you can fix Equity. I've seen you do it. You can fix anything. They're all on the make. I'll give you a few bob to help with the backhanders. I haven't been so excited since we torpedoed the Japanese flagship at the Medway do."

McHugh finished crunching his lunch and knocked back the glass of Rhineland white wine which Weldon Stack had provided. He decided to be cruel.

"Fred, you haven't got an atom of talent."

The engineer sat up straight and started laughing. He laughed so much that he fell off the scorched earth box. Weldon Stack noticed with distaste that Fred's socks were so saturated with oil and grease that they clung to his ankles like paint. Fred stopped laughing and wheezed awhile.

"I take it that we haven't dissuaded you?" Weldon Stack said coolly, his crooked mouth set.

"Look Weldon, we all deserve a chance to get out of the shit jobs. All my life I've been with bloody machines, watching them, listening to them. I've had machines up to here. They give nothing back. They're boring, dirty and you get no entertainment from them. I'm not one of these soft buggers who talk to them. Not me. I hate machines. Even when I was on the convoys going through to Murmansk I hated machines. What I want is some life, some colour! I want to give people a good time, take them out of themselves. All right, I'll say it, I want to hear that *applause*! I do! I'm honest about it! I want to see them out there! I want to give myself!"

Fred got to his feet and tweaked his nose. He was stirred by his own outgoing passion. Shuffling past Weldon Stack and McHugh he reached the door, paused, gave them both a sad, proud, dignified glance, then flung it open and stepped out into the sunlight.

Without words, the front-of-house manager and publicity manager/resident playwright agreed to register the engineer as having joined the ranks of the truly doomed.

five · Retreat of the Artist

McHugh stood on Sandra's doorstep with his travel-riter and a cardboard-box full of paper.

"I'm looking for some peace and quiet."

"Why are you looking here?" Sandra asked sardonically. "Is that all you want from me, peace and quiet?"

"I need somewhere to work. I keep getting interrupted at the theatre and my wife won't let me into the caravan."

"Do you want a bath as well as some peace and quiet?" Sandra asked, a glint in her grey eyes.

"All I want is a corner. I won't be a nuisance. You won't

know I'm here. Look Sandra, this is your chance to help my career as a writer. You said you were interested . . ."

Sandra beckoned McHugh to enter her lakeside mansion and ushered him into the kitchen where a coal fire was burning. She was still in her red silk dressing-gown and was half-way through her breakfast.

"Do you want some coffee?"

"I'd rather get started, if you don't mind."

"You can go in the front-room."

"The telephone is in there. If it rings it will stop the flow of inspiration. If you come in and start talking or reading a paper, I'll be disturbed again. What about the bathroom? I feel at ease there. You can use the downstairs toilet if you need to."

"Thanks, Ben."

"I could put that card-table up and use the lavatory seat. I like a wooden seat. Keeps the warmth."

"Whatever you say, Ben. Take the whole house over if you want. I only live here. If I want a bath I'll go and throw myself in the lake."

"And you've got to promise me that if you see Pilsudski you won't tell him where I'm hiding. That's essential. Put him on a false trail. Tell him I've gone somewhere else."

"To Harriet's?"

"No," McHugh said after a moment's thoughtfulness, "not to Harriet's."

"I know all about Harriet."

"So do I."

"And that Joan Earth woman. But I don't mind."

"Why should you mind?"

"Because I'm in love with you on the days when you come to see me. On those days I mind. The next day I don't mind at all. In fact I'm glad you've got other friends."

"I'd like to get started now. The play's in a critical stage of development. It is taking on a life of its own. The characters are emerging with an inner dynamism . . ."

"What's it about?"

"I don't want to talk about it."

"How the hell can I be interested in your work if you won't tell me anything about it? I think I've got a right to know what's going on in my own bathroom."

"It's about St Paul on the road to Damascus."

B

21

Sandra pulled her fluffy dark hair round her face like a frame and grimaced.

"That doesn't sound like you."

"I'm a very religious person at heart. Just because I have no formal faith it doesn't mean that I don't comprehend the mysteries of spiritual life. You can have visions without being a Christian. Take the cross for instance. What is the cross? Four legs. What does that symbolize?"

"Four legs?"

"Yes."

"Why is a cross four legs?"

"It's the four legs of the horse of God."

"I didn't know God had a horse."

"The horse of God is a symbol of his creative power."

"But a cross is four legs with no body."

"What is at the centre of the four points of the compass?"

"I don't know."

"The world. So what is at the end of the four legs of the cross?"

"I'll get you the card-table."

McHugh followed Sandra up the stairs into the bathroom and unfolded the card-table, put the wooden cover over the lavatory seat, took his travel-riter out of its case, opened his cardboard-box, and sat down.

"I'm glad the windows are frosted glass. It means I can't look out and get distracted."

"Ben," Sandra said, her slender hand on the door-ring. "Is it worth it?"

"Is what worth it?"

"Why not leave things as they are? Go back to being a personnel officer in the motor industry and forget about the horse of God? You'll be much happier. Out there the world is quite normal. It's only people like you who want to make it mad. Why do you goad things?"

McHugh smiled as he put the first sheet of bond, plus carbon and flimsy, in his travel-riter.

"If I told you that my whole life is one organic construction, that I draw heavily on my experience in the workaday world for my plays and poems, you wouldn't believe me, would you?"

McHugh laughed out loud and typed "Act Two Scene Three" at the top of the virgin sheet.

"If I told you that in this play I actually use an engine for a dramatic purpose, thereby establishing a positive connection between the motor industry and the theatre, would you believe me?"

"Ben, from you I would accept the news that Hitler was still alive and teaching in a British infants' school. I cannot be shocked any more."

"The double *deus ex machina*. St Paul on a horse of flesh and blood exactly mirrored by an engineer God on a mechanical horse powered by a generator."

"Ben, let's get in the bath. I understand getting in the bath."

"It works, Sandra, can't you see. It is pure theatre. No other medium could take it."

Sandra laughed grimly, examining her blue-painted nails.

"Ben, you're good for me. After I've had a conversation with you I have this tremendous urge to collect all the ordinary, normal, decent, sane people I know, put them in a room and just sit and listen to them talking about things like mortgages, inflation, babies falling out of prams, all the boring come-day-go-day crap I usually can't stand. You make me love normal mankind."

"Sandra, don't you think it might help our relationship if you took me seriously once in a while?" McHugh complained irritably. "Don't be so blasé."

Sandra managed a wintry smile before closing the door. As she went down the stairs the sound of typing ticked through the mansion like a giant death-watch beetle chewing at the foundations.

"That's impossible," Pilsudski said emphatically. "I'm not making this theatre into coterie entertainment for the rich. Haven't you got any social conscience, Sean? The Restoration was all over three hundred years ago. I'm not asking my actors to perform exclusively for any section of the community. That's immoral. If these middle-class creeps want to see *A Midsummer Night's Dream*, let them go to Stratford where they're appreciated and expected. This is a People's Theatre, not a plaything for the plutocracy."

"We're already committed . . ." Sean ground through clenched teeth.

"*You're* committed, Sean. You never consulted me. My

company will never, under any circumstances, humiliate themselves by doing shows under these kind of circumstances. We're not your jolly vagabonds."

Pilsudski glared over the first act of *The Blinding Light* at the general managers. Both of them were standing, having not been invited to sit down. Glenda's colour was scarlet, verging on puce. When she finally spoke her chin shook and her fat apple-shiny hands were tightly balled.

"Peter, Ed is a millionaire. If we do this for him he'll probably give us some money for next year's tour. All the people who will be going to the party are influential around here. As you know, there's a move to get Ben's play banned . . ."

"Christ, it's not written yet!" Pilsudski exploded. "What a prejudiced bunch of bastards!"

"I'm talking about *The Unfathomable Grass*," Glenda almost screamed. "They're saying it's obscene! The Leisure Committee have already voted to try and get the police to prosecute!"

"And you think that if we do a special idyllic performance of *Dream* for these ponces then they'll leave Ben alone? You're crazy. We know that it's Beryl who keeps ringing up the police about the play and trying to get them to prosecute. She's a crank. This has been going on for weeks."

"Peter," Sean said as calmly as he could, "we are throwing away thousands of pounds. You have to make allowances in this business. It's no good thinking you can survive without the help of the local authority and the people who matter . . ."

"You mean the Orrestwater Mafia?" Pilsudski snorted. "Tell them to go and screw themselves. I'm making no compromises with snobs, shitheads or sycophants, and that includes you two. Get out of my office."

"If that's going to be your attitude I've got no alternative. I'm now *instructing* you to stage this performance. I have that right. I'm the general manager . . ."

Glenda nudged Sean.

"Sorry, we're the general manager and we administer the business side. This is business. It's public relations. If McHugh was doing his job properly he'd be behind us in this. Doing the *Dream* on the island can do us nothing but good."

Pilsudski pored over his script. In his green eyes there gleamed a calculating, penetrating light.

"All right, Sean. We'll do it," he said eventually. "And congrats on Glenda's promotion."

"Well, it's only acting at the moment. The board have got to approve of the new post, but I expect they'll agree. They usually take my advice."

Pilsudski nodded and let it be seen that he considered the confrontation to be over. As Sean and Glenda backed towards the door the artistic director raised his head again.

"I'll go along with you Sean providing you don't try to interfere with Ben's new play. If you try to screw up *The Blinding Light*, then the island deal is off, and I'll oppose your latest bit of nepotism."

"I don't know what you're talking about," Sean declared stoutly, giving Glenda his hand as she stepped down the wooden planks to the ground. "You know we like to encourage talent as much as you."

"Where's Ben?" Joan Earth breathed to Weldon Stack. "I must get in touch with him."

"He wants to be left alone to finish the play. He's only got three days."

Joan Earth knew that there was no point in being voluptuous to the front-of-house manager. He did not like women of Joan's build but preferred them to be all eyelashes and nipples. Joan towered over Weldon Stack's concept of sexuality. He thought that there was enough of Joan to be shared out among a dozen men with some left over. Yet he recognized her talent as a particular kind of actress and knew that she would get to the top. One day Joan Earth's name would be up in lights in Shaftesbury Avenue or St Martin's Lane and her photographs would appear along the sides of the escalators of the London underground railway system. He had her down on his list of potential successes and did not want to turn her away without offering some kind of help.

"I can get a message to him."

"Then you know where he is?"

"I didn't say that."

"Weldon, would you think I was awful if I told you that I want to influence Ben to write me a nice part?"

"Not at all. He thinks very highly of you."

"I know that. But I'm talking about my acting. Ben could

write me a lovely part if he put his mind to it. That's all I want to see him for."

"I admire your frankness, Joan."

"I thought you'd understand, Weldon. Don't you find there's a strange kind of telepathy between us? Nothing physical. Only the mind."

"It's my job to interpret the needs of theatre people as well as the public. Would you be shocked if I offered you a deal?"

"Not at all, it would make things much easier. I would know where I stood."

"I am willing to reveal to you where Ben is hiding providing you will fulfil the following requirements. First, that you won't tell him I told you. Second, you will not cause a scene when you find out that he is with another woman. Third, you will take my brother under your wing when he arrives from Ottawa and do what you can for him."

Joan took a deep breath.

"What's your brother like?"

Weldon Stack paused, thoughtful.

"I have known people who liked him."

"Many people?"

"Enough to convince me that he can be liked, if you take my point."

"Do you like him?"

"He is my brother. I love him. Not only that, he is my *elder* brother which means that I have a proper idea of his status."

"And you want me to be his friend? You know I'm not too bright Weldon. Is your brother an educated and civilized man like yourself? Would you say that about him?"

Weldon Stack paused again, even more thoughtful.

"He's a *cultured* man, but a man of very pressing impulses and instincts . . ." the front-of-house manager explained gently. "He's a sensualist."

"I understand, Weldon. I think my side of the telepathy needs more imagination. Where is Ben?"

"You agree?"

"Of course."

Weldon Stack betrayed the whereabouts of his friend without unease or emotion. The balance of power was being maintained and the game was entering a new dimension. By

26

the opening night of *The Blinding Light* there could be a radical improvement in Weldon Stack's prospects, or his gamble would have failed. The human element would decide which way the pendulum swung, the human element, that most fascinating clay in the hands of the master-potter of destinies, Weldon Stack.

## six · Literary Pursuits

Over the past weeks Beryl had telephoned the sergeant at the desk of the Orrestwater police station so often about her husband's play that they had struck up a relationship. That afternoon Beryl went through her list of bachelors in the staff-room of the remedial school and gave them all a thorough scrutiny. None of them was absolutely foolproof. Above all she must have a standard, reliable, plain man who would not go off at tangents which would end up in places like the Dramacart Moving Theatre Company. Only a year ago Beryl had been firmly established on a private housing estate just outside Liverpool with McHugh going off to work at seven-thirty each morning and dropping Beryl off at the gates of a girls' grammar school. Their joint income was over four thousand pounds and McHugh had received an invitation from the Round Table to join their ranks. The decline had started with McHugh buying the travel-riter to do work at home, reports and projects for the personnel manager of the factory where he worked. Within a month he had given up his job, sold the house, rejected the Protestant work ethic, and joined the Dramacart, dragging the griping Beryl along with him. Everyone in the family had condemned the move as foolish. McHugh was doomed to certain failure in an ignoble profession. Of all the arts, Beryl saw writing as the most fraudulent and untrustworthy. All writers were liars. They could not be trusted. They twisted reality into their own shapes. They would not accept life as it *was*. To do that needed courage and intelligence. Even to be a success as a writer was to admit failure. It simply meant that the public had accepted the writer's toys as their own. With all this in her mind Beryl consciously took a decision to fall in love with the sergeant at the police station. If there was stability and sense to be found in Orrestwater, that's where it was located. What divorce court could fail to be impressed with an adultery action which involved an officer of the Law? Beryl would get everything that was left in the savings account with the Bradford & Bingley Building Society. The sergeant would get a police semi-detached with a blue light over the door. Life could start again.

"I wondered if I could see you again to discuss this?" Beryl said over the telephone from the corner of the staff-room.

"Obscenity is a difficult thing to prove. I told you . . ."

"Would you take me out for a drink?"

"After school?"

"I enjoyed our last chat. I made the third form write an essay in French on obscenity in the cinema."

The sergeant said "oh" at the other end of the line. There was a difficult pause.

"I tell you what," the burly grizzled officer of the Law said gruffly, but not without warmth. "There's an old friend of mine has asked me to a party tonight, sounds just right. She says it's her Celebration Of Normality party, whatever that is. She's just been in. I've done her a few favours in my time so I reckon she won't mind me bringing you along. How about it?"

Beryl nearly cried with delight.

"That sounds like just the kind of party I need. Oh please take me. I can't wait."

"Where shall I pick you up, Borrans Field?"

"No, not there. Where's the house we're going to?"

"It's a big place down by the lake."

"Couldn't I meet you outside?"

"I suppose so."

The sergeant gave Beryl instructions how to get to Sandra's Celebration Of Normality party and arranged to meet her at the imposing granite-acorned entrance at half-past eight.

It was the twenty-first telephone call that had come through since Sandra left the house, leaving McHugh working in the bathroom. All Sandra's friends were the kind of people who hang on for several minutes, letting the telephone ring in case someone comes in. McHugh tore the sheet of paper out of the travel-riter and ran down the stairs.

"What?" he bellowed into the mouthpiece.

The chief biologist at the Freshwater Research Station stepped back from the instrument.

"Come on, what do you want?" McHugh screamed.

"I'm looking for Sandra."

"If you're looking for Sandra what the fuck are you doing on the telephone? Get out and organize a man-hunt. Goodbye."

"Who are you?"

"I'm the butler."

"You're a very rude butler."

"That's how she likes her butlers."

The chief biologist explained that he was only ringing up to ask Sandra if he could bring one of his juniors to the party that evening. He could vouch for the fact that she was normal.

"What party? There's going to be no party here. I'm hard at work. I've got to have peace and quiet."

"I thought butlers were interested in parties, showing people in and taking round drinks on a tray."

"Look, there's butlers and butlers. I'm an introspective and dinner-for-one butler. I'm putting the phone down right now."

"Are you coming to the party?"

"Which party?"

"The party at Sandra's place tonight. I must say I don't think you should be. You don't sound very normal to me."

McHugh replaced the receiver, went upstairs and packed up his equipment. Five minutes later he was walking across the garden to the lake.

Two air-hostesses and a fork-lift truck driver carried Jules Stack from the aircraft and tried to make him stand on the tarmac. He refused, deliberately buckling his knees as his feet touched the ground, clutching at the necks of his bearers in panic.

"You're at Manchester now, sir, you've arrived," one of the air-hostesses said with a jaded attempt at brightness and conviviality. "It's all over."

Jules groaned and hung on to them.

"Just one mistake and it could have been all over. Bring me another brandy will you?"

"Sir, we've landed. You're outside the aircraft now. We've stopped serving drinks."

"Have we had lunch? I didn't get my little plastic bottle of wine. Don't look at me like that! I didn't, dammit! You passed me by. And the main course was lousy. What was it? Elk? Christ, I feel terrible. Have you got any bicarb? Where's the cheese? And I want real cheese, with port. What year is the port? I don't give a damn, any year will do. Got any Ottawa Oloroso for before breakfast?"

"Sir, we have to leave you now. It's only a hundred yards to the airport building. Take a few deep breaths . . ."

"What d'ya want to do? Kill me? Look nurse, please tell me when we're coming down. That's the worst part, the descent."

"Sir, we're on the ground. This is terra firma."

"I can't wait around here all day," said the fork-lift truck driver, leaving go of his side, "I've got a job to do."

Jules Stack slid to the tarmac. One of the air-hostesses put his stick in his hand and rested his Ottawa Outangs ice-hockey team white plastic overnight bag by his side. They could do no more for the confused composer. During the trip they had marvelled at the stamina of the strange, shock-haired, hound-faced man with the bottle-end glasses who had drunk forty-seven brandies and soda crossing the Atlantic and poked at the trim, tight buttocks of the air-hostesses with the rubber end of his silver-topped stick. He did not go to sleep during the flight, or stop talking. By the time the plane had cleared the Canadian east coast there were ten empty seats around Jules Stack and several passengers were lying in the aisle rather than have anything to do with him.

"It's all right. I'll take over from here," Weldon Stack said briskly as he climbed off the motorized baggage trolley which he had borrowed from a subornable porter. "Hello, Jules. Long time no see."

"Jeeeezus, now I'm hearing voices, nurse. I distinctly heard that bastard my little brother talking. Can you get me another handful of those carmine and green capsules?"

Weldon Stack persuaded the air-hostesses to help him load his overtired sibling on to the baggage trolley and drove it back into the airport building. He had already fixed Jules's entrance to Great Britain with both customs and immigration, using a contact in the Home Office who had been in the same form as his at Winchester. Stopping the baggage trolley beside the Dramacart Land-Rover he called to Bert who was reading the *Daily Mirror* in the driving-seat to give him a hand.

"Another fookin intellectual," Bert grumbled, glancing down.

"Don't forget his stick."

"What does he need a stick for? I thought you said he was only thirty? I must say he looks nearer fookin fifty."

Bert's observation was not without foundation. The sufferings of the creative artist were carved on Jules Stack's face as gullies and channels are carved by the seas on chalk cliffs. Behind his bottle-end spectacles were eyes that had seen the bottoms of a thousand pits. Grey streaks were in his hair already and the veins in his nose were dull scarlet threads and tiny indigo knots.

With his brother securely cushioned against the jolts of the journey, Weldon Stack got in beside Bert and signalled him to drive off. Music, the most immediate beauty in the arts, was being carried north.

Jules groaned deeply from the back of the vehicle.

"Why bring me to England? It doesn't seem right. I ran away once."

"You need a change, Jules. Do some work. A fresh start."

"Look Weldon, I'm the older brother. I should organize *you*."

"You do, Jules. I spend half my life worrying about what's happening to you. Doesn't that count? If you're here then I'll know what you're up to. Why did you assault the viola player at the German Embassy's New Year party?"

"He was putting grace notes in the lower registers."

"Don't you think it's about time you wrote your music instead of living it?"

"Weldon, get off my back for Chrissake. Who put the suspension in this buggy? Shipbuilders? I've given up music. I don't want to compete. They murdered me over there. You can't create in a country with licensing laws like they've got. What am I coming home to? Two hours drinking on Sunday afternoons. Closed at ten-thirty. I won't have a chance. I'll bet you a dollar to a handful of horse-shit that Winnipeg Wineries don't have retail outlets over here. How can I survive?"

Weldon turned and smiled at Jules, stretching a hand down to pat his jolting shoulder.

"We'll hear the Stack music again. It's in you Jules."

"Got anything to eat?"

Weldon Stack deftly undid the buckle on a wicker hamper behind his seat. To the delight of his elder brother he then produced a cold chicken, a loaf of farmhouse bread, a Waldorf salad, half a pound of Lancashire medium tasty cheese, a blackberry and apple pie, a pot of Gentleman's Relish and four bottles of Riesling in a plastic waste-paper basket full of cracked ice.

"Just for the journey, Jules," Weldon murmured as he rooted for the salted creamery butter and cutlery. "I knew you'd need a snack before we got to Orrestwater and a decent meal."

"Got any celery to go with the cheese?"

Weldon bit his lip.

"I'm sorry, Jules, old man. I forgot."

"Keerist, isn't that just typical of you? You can't control the detail. Can't you do anything properly? It burns my ass when you're so sloppy."

"Sorry, Jules. We can stop on the way."

"There're no vegetable stalls on the fookin motorway," Bert muttered. "All I had for my dinner was a potato pie."

"We can make a detour," Weldon Stack insisted gently. "Try the centre of Manchester. We're sure to find celery there."

"Where's Ben?"

Pilsudski took Joan Earth aside during a break in an improvisation session. The actors and actresses were imagining that they were about to be publicly hanged and had been asked to put together a little mime and farewell speech from the scaffold. Joan Earth had given a very telling performance. All the men in the company had been close to hysteria when they contemplated such a waste. Joe Woodhead had gone outside for some fresh air, fighting back the tears of frustration.

"I don't know."

"Joan . . ." Pilsudski said warningly. "No lies. You and I have got to be absolutely straight with each other. I can't work with deceit. It puts up obstacles to a true understanding between director and actor. You've got to trust me."

"Tell my mother that I spoke her name at the last . . ."

Pilsudski asked Murphy Winspear to hold on for a moment while he finished talking to Joan. Murphy flounced off right and half-hid himself behind the curtain. Sex was at the root of everything in this company. That was Murphy Winspear's opinion. After twenty years in the business he could not tolerate the heterosexual monopoly any longer.

"If I tell you, will you give me the part that Ben asks you to give me?" Joan smiled winningly, stroking her long black hair. He'll *design* it for me, you'll be miscasting if you give it to anyone else."

"Joan, how can you?" Pilsudski grated. "You're making me cry with shame."

"Peter, I've got to think of myself."

"Christ, Joan, I'd like to get you on a sheep-station at shearing-time when it's a hundred degrees in the shade. You Poms are so corrupt the vultures won't come here, even for their holidays. There are times when I wish I was back on the Great Barrier Reef with a piece of string and a bent pin."

"Ready for me now Peter dearie?" Murphy Winspear smiled with acid sweetness as he prepared himself to face the drop to eternity. "I can't hang around here all day."

As Murphy Winspear gingerly stepped on to the trap Pilsudski nodded blackly at the leading lady of *The Blinding Light*, or her who would be so if its writer was still susceptible to the reasoning powers of lust.

At six o'clock, opening-time, Sandra began touring all the public houses in Orrestwater to find normal people to invite to her party. She calculated that many tradesmen, lawyers, bankers, boilermakers and bus drivers went in to a bar straight after work so they could have a few drinks and then go home to spend the major part of the evening with their wives and children watching the television or playing Monopoly. These were the type of normal people she wanted. The ones who went straight home after work, bolted their dinner after a cat's lick-and-a-promise in the bathroom, and went out to the public houses until closing time would probably include many of the abnormal people whom Sandra wanted to avoid as far as her party was concerned. After an hour of inviting normal people and being politely refused because they were normal people who thought it was abnormal to be invited to a party for normal people by a woman they didn't know, Sandra entered the saloon bar of the Dog and Pheasant and looked around. The only other customer was a shock-haired man with pebble glasses who appeared to be very tired. Hooked on to the bar by his side was a silver-topped stick.

"I suppose you're having a quiet drink before going home to a frozen steak and kidney pie, frozen peas and frozen chips and an evening with your lovely family."

Jules Stack, for it was he, looked up from his pint of beer.

"That I am lady. Just lead me to it."

"A hard day at the office?"

"You've no goddamned idea. It was sheer hell."

"I'm having a little get-together for normal people at my house down by the lake tonight. Would you like to come?"

"For normal people?"

"That's right."

"Do you guarantee that only normal people will be there? I'm of a very nervous disposition."

"I've only invited normal people. You'll be all right."

"Would you happen to have a piano?"

"Yes, a Steiner baby grand. I've just had it tuned. Can you play?"

"Only normal music."

"That's what I want."

"Say, is this a bottle-party?"

"Good heavens no. I'm providing the drink. That's normal isn't it? I mean, only abnormal people throw parties when they can't afford it."

"That's very true," Jules Stack affirmed.

"Then you'll come?"

"With pleasure."

"May I know your name?"

There was a pause. Jules Stack stared into his beer and pushed out his lower lip.

"Frank Williams. That's a pretty normal name isn't it?"

"Perfect."

"Are you going home now?"

Sandra looked at her watch.

"I think I better had. I've got a lot to do before my guests

arrive. I've said half-past eight, which is the most normal
time I could think of and I suppose, as they're all normal
people, they'll arrive at ten to nine."

"Would you think it was abnormal of me to ask if I could
come back with you now, give a hand with the arrangements
and play your piano?"

Sandra gave Frank Williams a quizzing with her sophisticated and woman-of-the-world eyes.

"What about your family?"

"I'm away from home. Jeeeezus, how I miss the little
woman and the kids! I think even abnormal people hate
hotel lounges, don't they?"

"One more question. I can tell from your accent that
you're not English. I'm prepared to agree that there are
normal people outside England, but where do you come
from?"

"Canada lady. I assure you, it's the dullest country in the
world. If you come from Canada you *have* to be normal."

## seven · Two Journeys

Sean drove Glenda to Icklington station in their jointly-
owned Volkswagen. Not only did they find that it was a
remarkably economic little car to run but its finely en-
gineered German motor cruised like a sewing-machine on
the low-grade petrol which they siphoned out of the enormous tanks on the Thorneycroft. As they joined the traffic
jam in Curdog they fell to discussing the itinerary for
Glenda's visit to the metropolis. She was going to stay in
Hampstead with Rhoda Pearson's mother who, in turn, had
asked Dearden Ryan and Geoffrey Block of the Theatrefund
over to dinner. Before dinner Glenda would go to the
Spaniard's Inn, the Flask, Sir Richard Steele's and the Horse
and Groom to contact all the other influential executives of
the national grant-aid body in order to warn them about
what Pilsudski was doing with the Dramacart and to gain
their support for her elevation. She would apprise them of
the situation in the fullest possible detail, especially with
reference to McHugh who had recently applied for a bursary.

"See how the land lies love, don't push too hard. You know

how they change their allegiances every five minutes. De-
scribe what we know of *The Blinding Light* to them and try
to get a reaction. All right? See if you can get authority for
us to appoint a new assistant manager in your place. If I
offered that to Weldon I'm sure he'd come in with us and
get off the fence . . ."

Sean parked outside the station and carried Glenda's pig-
skin briefcase and beadwork shoulder-satchel on to the platform after purchasing her a first-class ticket and handing her
five pounds for a British Rail dinner. When the train came in
he got on board and found her a seat in a compartment that
was empty except for an old lady who was sound asleep.
One glance at the paperback book on her knees, *Mushroom-
Growing For Profit*, was sufficient to assure him that she was
a fit companion for his partner.

Glenda came to the door to say good-bye. As the train
was pulling out, Sean reached up and pressed the engagement
ring into Glenda's hand, then stepped back to allow himself
to be enveloped in the pouring, romantic steam from the
mighty pistons—a scene he vividly recalled from an old film
which had touched him deeply. As he waited for the mysterious shroud to swirl around his rugged and composed features
he remembered that the line had been electrified and shrank
away towards the exit, hardly daring to glance down the
platform at the glowing red moon of his beloved who was
beaming back at him from the retreating carriage.

McHugh tramped up the quarry road with his travel-riter
and cardboard-box of paper. Behind him the long green dale
fell away into flat pastures flanked by low hills and the
rushing torrent of the River Sprint eased into slow curves,
pools and flood-plains. Ahead of him the bright water coursed
and leapt through gorges and over precipices as if pursued
by the early summer moon. He wished that he had sneaked
back to the Dramacart to see if Fred had put the silencer on
his car but the chances were that Pilsudski had got the
engineer working on converting the Perkins into a mechanical horse as a number one priority and that was a project
which would take the marine engineer considerable time
and ingenuity. At least he would have it ready for the first
read-through. From the way the play was developing it was
clear that the role of the generator was of primary import-

ance. McHugh had read through the Book of Revelations of St John the Divine for some help in the structure of a sub-text and had encountered the Four Horsemen, friends of many a novelist, poet and visionary. McHugh would have preferred One Horseman to go with St Paul. The quartet of riders was overcrowding his mind. Pilsudski would never be able to get five horses on the Dramacart stage. It had no wing-space or fly-space and measured twenty feet across the proscenium width and had only eighteen feet of depth. Trying to pack five quadrupeds into that space would be like trying to get a quart into a pint pot. Not only that, there would be the noise problem and the question of defecation. The Perkins would not defecate but the other four, at some time in the run, would certainly defecate. In mid-summer, in a confined space with an inadequate ventilation system, the result could be disastrous. What would happen if the horses defecated on the night when the West End impresarios came up from London? The opening night, when the *Guardian* and the *Daily Telegraph* were there, searching for an opportunity to be ironical or poisonous? They were all blind and sour, these critics. There was no chance that they would be able to see beyond the immediate image of five horses stamping about on the rickety stage of the Dramacart and defecating, to the universal truths and majestic symbols of Life and Death which currently rolled around in McHugh's dreaming brain. With an inner sigh, he disposed of the Four Horsemen of the Apocalypse and sent them galloping back into the fantastic mind of the strange saint who had invented them. Better to stick to good old St Paul and the Perkins.

McHugh reached the derelict slate-quarry and found a spot out of the wind where he could build himself a table of slates to type on. The only sounds were those of sleepy larks making their last ascents and the baa of distant sheep. Below these sounds, the Sprint sang a deep, rushing song.

Within minutes the derelict slate-quarry carried a new instrument in its evening orchestra. The tapping of a solitary percussion piece, a ripple of *a*s and *b*s and *c*s, a flurry of question marks and colons, the drum of Ben McHugh.

Glenda looked in the mirror of the rocking compartment and carefully tied the shoe-lace around her neck, positioned the engagement ring under her chin, then snapped shut the top of her turtle-necked orlon shepherd's smock. The ring made a little bump. It occurred to Glenda that she might be better advised to keep the ring in her bag but sentiment and the fear of being attacked in the London streets by desperate drug-addicts and football-fans who might snatch the bag away, made Glenda choose this safe and clandestine way of wearing Sean's token of their love. She was confident that Sean would understand why she could not wear it on her finger. The wearing of such bourgeois talismans was not approved of in Hampstead these days. It would only take one report of Glenda's erring ostentation to reach the Theatrefund and the entire grant to the Dramacart would be withdrawn. As it was, the brave and chummy relationship between the co-general managers, living in worthy sin in their purple caravan, was a garland round the brows of the ramshackle contraption of the mobile theatre. There could be no pointing of fingers. No accusations of preserving theatre for a middle-class audience and excluding the giant culture-hungry masses. Yet, beneath the synthetic wool of her garment, those precious jewels would keep the burning light, warmed by her own well-bred blood. With a possessive pat at the bump Glenda sat down and opened her book, *Terra-cotta Objects of the Home Counties*, and turned to her place, holding the Beatrix Potter parchment marker betwixt finger and thumb as she read.

"Would you like to guess exactly how old I am?"

Glenda started. She had thought that the old woman was still asleep. Two bright, inquisitive eyes met hers from a face of indefinable age. Her hair was snow white and the flesh around her nose and eyes was pale and peaky. She could have been a hundred.

Glenda smiled the smile she allocated to the patients of the mental hospitals when they came to the Dramacart for their annual treat and fought with each other over the last chocolate ice-cream in the usherette's tray.

"Well, that's very hard to say . . ." she began.

"Past ninety you'd think eh? I'm not. I'm not even sixty. I'll be fifty-nine next March. What do you think of that?" the old woman sniffed, flipping her mushroom book shut. "It's *his* fault."

"Oh," Glenda said wisely.

"Don't you have any children. Don't do it. It's not worth it. Die curious dear."

"Has the coffee been round yet?"

"Don't change the subject."

Glenda glanced at her watch. There was another hour before dinner.

"You're not interested are you? Your sort never are. I know people like you. The sympathy vote. You want to try growing mushrooms in Carlisle. That was *his* idea of course. I wish his father was alive. He'd knock some sense into him."

"Is this your husband you're talking about?" Glenda inquired, conscious of the danger she was letting herself in for, the old woman being obviously geared up for a tremendous session of autobiography.

"No, thank God. At least by being his mother I escaped from being his wife. That burden is on another pair of shoulders dear, not mine. God help the girl. She deserves a medal. If I was her I'd leave him flat and go into a nunnery. They're not worth it. Don't get married. You might end up with someone like my son."

"As a matter of fact I am getting married, quite soon."

"Just check to see it's no one like *him*. Have the feller examined by a psychiatrist. If there's anything in him that resembles my boy, run like hell. If you don't, you might as well chuck yourself under a bus."

Glenda was becoming intrigued. She examined the old woman with a new interest. Above her, on the luggage-rack, was a case with a label. It was turned in such a way that Glenda could only see the last two letters of the surname— *gh*.

"Don't ask me where he gets it from. It's not me and it's not his father. I suppose we should have realized what we were in for long ago. What a child he was, still is. He used to put his shoes and socks down the drain. Now that's Freudian isn't it? That's what his grandfather said. Freudian. He didn't stop wetting the bed till he was thirteen. I caught him standing on the head-board actually doing it, wide-awake one morning. What kind of mind do you think that is? School? Don't talk to me about school. Those poor teachers. They earn every penny they get. If I'd been one of his teachers I'd have paid the other kids to kick him to pieces. We had a nice house in the suburbs, grass along the side of the avenue, smashing furniture from Blacklers, and I kept it clean. Every day I polished that house from top to bottom. We were in a nice class of people. The feller over the road was the manager at Pegram's. The feller next door was a foreman joiner at Cammell Laird's. We had three executives in the avenue. No noise after nine o'clock. We were getting somewhere. Except for *him*. He didn't appreciate it."

"Would you say you were lower middle-class?" Glenda asked.

"No dear, definitely *nouveau riche*! Definitely *nouveau riche*! When my husband died he was worth thousands. You should have seen my gas stove. Not that *he* tried to behave accordingly. When he got married I heaved a sigh of relief. She was such a nice level-headed girl. I sat in the church and cried my eyes out for her. For a couple of years I thought she'd done the trick. He got a good job. Got a mortgage on a nice house, not quite as good as ours but *new*, with central-heating. She was working as well. Then he suddenly chucks it all up and says he can't abide it all. That was my bad luck. My husband had left our house to this idiot and asked him to let me stay there until I passed on. Not him. He throws me out into the street and sets me up in a freezing place up in Carlisle growing mushrooms with some of the money he got from the sale of the house. Now he's wandering around saying he's a writer, spending what's left of the money and driving poor Beryl out of her mind with worry. All we can hope for is they'll lock him up. He'll do something bad, I know him."

Glenda controlled an instinct to throw her arms around the old woman and kiss her. Not since the day that she had asked Rhoda Pearson to put a word in for her with Mr Kel in order to get the box-office job six months ago had good fortune shone upon Glenda with such phenomenal benevolence. Here was the evidence she needed. With beating heart she stood up and craned her neck to look at the baggage-label. It was. Oh, it was! It was!

"Mrs McHugh, would you allow me to buy you some dinner?" she said, eyes dancing with pleasure. "It will shorten the journey for both of us."

"As long as it's anything but mushrooms," the mother of

the artist replied, getting to her feet. "I can't stand the bloody things."

It was going well. In the fading light the lonely figure rattled away at his travel-riter, the words flowing like the Sprint below, his mind spiralling upwards in thermals of thought to where the kestrels hovered in their vole-hunting. St Paul had emerged now. He was alive. The doubter, the fascist, the pogromist, the almighty lover of God Perkins, the great apostle of the Word and opponent of the Flesh. Titatic battles raged in the breast of this man. He was the battlefield of ideologies and empires, and all in song. Songs poured from the flashing aluminium key-heads, verse after verse, gifts for the unknown composer, the colleague in creation who would re-fire them in another, compatible beauty. McHugh was transported. He imagined the old steel box resounding with his lyrics, complementing the mountain winds and the bubbling whistles of the birds. It was not all ecstasy though, this play. It had its sombre moments and agonies. There was a balance which reflected the true rhythms of human life. There were peaks and troughs. He had abjured the use of the King James the First Bible language and only used contemporary idiom, but it was re-forged into a dialect of dignity, colour and glittering perception, a diamond chisel to carve anew the shape of Man out of the mountainside. Through this medium the Acts of the Apostles lived again, the clank and whirr of God Perkins harmonizing with the march of Roman sandals. It was sheer technical expertise and a piercing insight into the inner mechanism of the dimension of Time which gave McHugh the initiative to render chapter nine verse five of the Acts from:

> And he said, Who art thou Lord?
> And the Lord said, I am Jesus whom
> Thou persecutest: it is hard for
> thee to kick against the pricks.

to:

SAUL OF TARSUS (St Paul) (screams) My eyes! Argh, my eyes! Turn out that light! Caesar, save me! Dear emperor, douse that light!

GOD PERKINS I fire on all four cylinders of the Apocalypse.

SAUL OF TARSUS (St Paul) (shaking all over) What is this
  Lazarus-beam which bores into my soul from the centre
  of your forehead?
GOD PERKINS That is the Prime Mover crystal in my equine
  brain.
SAUL OF TARSUS (St Paul) Why burn me up? Leave me my
  mind, oh please leave me my power of Reason!
GOD PERKINS (singing) *Thi-i-i-i-s is the hour*
                        *Of h-o-r-s-e power.*

"He's not working class at all like he claims. He's *nouveau
riche*. I got it from the most reliable source. Met his mother
on the train. It stuck out a mile. I tell you, Ben McHugh is a
phoney right through. You should hear the values that his
mother maintains. God, it would make you sick to listen to
her. He's got no real roots in the working class at all. He's
a typical child of the *nouveaux riches*, irresponsible, spoilt,
assuming political sympathies which he doesn't sincerely
believe in. He's on the make! He's using the Dramacart as a
stepping-stone. I think it's a cynical rotten business, he's
exploiting Pilsudski . . ."

Dearden Ryan stroked his spade beard and fiddled with
the reveres of his plum-coloured corduroy jacket.

"This is a very serious allegation, Glenda. McHugh is being
considered for a bursary at the moment. We can't give
bursaries to the scions of the *nouveaux riches*. Isn't there
any semblance of working-class honesty or well-tried virtues
in the man? Surely there's one redeeming feature . . ."

"Never mind the bursary, Dearden," Glenda said, dismis-
sing the issue as being beyond consideration. "You can't give
him that now. What we want to know is how to get rid of
him. Poor Pilsudski is his slave. All McHugh has to do is say
he wants to write another play and Peter just pulls another
show out of the repertoire. I think it's some kind of hold
that McHugh has over him. They could be queers . . . er, you
know . . . liberated . . ." Glenda faltered.

Geoffrey Block frowned, sniffing the perfume on his lace
cuffs.

"What's that got to do with it?"

"All I'm saying is that the *motives* are wrong. The Dramacart is being abused by people who have no real concern for
its welfare. Sean and I worked our fingers to the bone just to

keep the old thing on the move, doing its job, carrying the torch . . ."

"All right, Glenda, we know you do a wonderful job. Let's stick to the problem. What can we do? Look, I realize that what you are saying about McHugh's background is absolutely damning. We were prepared to overlook the fact that he'd been working in the motor industry and had never drawn unemployment benefit, been part of a commune or said fuck on television but this new evidence . . . wow . . . I don't know what to say . . ."

Dearden Ryan looked at his colleague for help. They had to give Glenda something to take back to Sean. She had to have hope that the Dramacart would be relieved from the army of the Devil camped at its gates.

"I think we'll have to come up and have a look for ourselves," Geoffrey sighed as he bit into a chocolate mint finger. "Have a quiet little unofficial investigation. I suppose it had better be tomorrow, Dearden, even though it means we'll miss Jimmy Threyn-Tomlinson's lovely ceramic show in the foyer of the National Film Theatre. What a pity. Too bad, we have our jobs to do in the wilderness. Heigh-ho. At least we'll get some fresh air."

Glenda beamed with gratitude.

It was exactly what she had hoped for.


## eight · The Knocking of the Norm

Sandra was bewildered. Throughout the rooms of her lakeside mansion she was discovering her guests hunting for the normal people whom they had heard were being invited to this party. They searched everywhere, passing each other in halls and corridors with drinks in hand and calling out queries as to whether anyone had found one yet. Sandra did her best. She gave these normal guests accusing stares which were supposed to nail them to the floorboards with guilt, but she had no success. Her normal guests presumed that she was looking through them or over their shoulders at the phantom normal people who were supposed to be the centre-piece of the celebrations. Only one guest was admitting that he was normal. He sat at the keyboard of the Steiner baby grand, his hound-face radiant, eyes swimming behind the pebble glasses, striking enormous chords and intervals other than unison, octave, perfect fifth and fourth, major and minor third and sixth and their octaves, ripping off dissonant trills and crashing the piano lid up and down while pounding the polished brass pedals with his feet. Sandra was beginning to have doubts about Frank Williams. She was a long way behind the other normal guests who had, with incisive insight, seen that Frank Williams was drunk as well as normal. Sandra had noticed that during the course of the early evening while Frank Williams had been helping her to lay out the rooms with drinks and snacks, two of the six bottles of whisky had disappeared along with a full carton of Long Life beer cans and a flagon of Old English cider.

"For Chrissake, am I the only normal person here?" Jules Stack roared, whirling round on the piano-stool to face a bunch of chuckling guests who were observing his antics. "I've been let down! Sandra, where's my friends, the nice normal people?"

"We're all nice normal people here, Frank, aren't we?"

Sandra smiled appealingly at her guests who doubled up with laughter at the idea that any one of them was boring enough to be normal.

"Pity that guy did a bunk from the bathroom, the abnormal guy. I would like to have met him. Did he have horns and a tail?" Jules Stack cackled, his usually grey countenance mottled with red patches.

"Yes," replied Sandra with feeling.

"Well, what are we going to do?"

It was the chief biologist from the Freshwater Research Station who spoke. Like all the others, he had accepted the invitation to come to the Celebration Of Normality party as an outsider, much as an atheist will creep into High Mass just to see what goes on. Now it had been established that there were no normal people who had actually turned up, it was necessary that the party should be abnormal in character in order to prove beyond doubt that those who had arrived should have a strong claim to being outside the normal normal classification. This meant that no one could put on any of their golden oldie records, get haplessly drunk, talk loudly about their pet hates, or take other normal people off to the bedrooms for a quick screw. This was all part of the normal pattern of behaviour at parties and was therefore out.

"We're stymied," the chief biologist complained. "What can we do?"

"Look you guys, I'm normal and you're abnormal. If you do the exact opposite of what I do, then you'll be fine. Let me get on with this dreary business of being normal and you just enjoy yourselves in your abnormal way," Frank Williams advised them wisely. "Be contrary for Chrissake!"

"I'm not sure that I'm willing to be thought of as abnormal," observed a tall thin woman who was the manager of the local tannery, "but I would admit to being *different*. Wouldn't you fellows go along with that?"

The other guests murmured their agreement that they would rather be thought of as different rather than as abnormal. They awaited the pianist's reply with interest.

"Are we saying that there is a sliding scale of normalcy?" Frank Williams asked donnishly. "Would that cover your reservations? Then you can take your pick where the god-damned hell you want to be on the scale. Me? I'm at the normal end, a normal kinda guy playing the piano in a normal way."

The other guests cast lingering glances over the composer's ashen, pickled countenance. Tonight they had reason enough to be smug about being so different. The tannery manager stroked her faint moustache and watched Jules Stack/Frank Williams rip his pulverizing hands along the octaves and smash his unfeeling knuckles into the wooden end of the keyboard. Smiling widely he looked up, waved his hands in the air and fell off the stool. Once on the blue floral Wilton carpet he doubled up and puked accurately between the brass pedals.

"You try doing that," he challenged the different guests. "I suppose you have to fail, not being normal. Doesn't it make you feel left out?"

As the police sergeant was dragging Jules Stack up the oak staircase, satisfied that at last he had found something that was genuinely and legally obscene, the massive front door reverberated with heavy knocking. Sandra, half-stupefied by the fate of her sitting-room carpet, opened it and found Pilsudski, Weldon Stack and Joan Earth on the doorstep. Jules Stack glanced down and saw the corporeal glory beneath him, broke free of the police sergeant, fell down the stairs and threw himself on Joan Earth, his pianist's hands groping. When the police sergeant had re-made his arrest and hauled the mumbling ex-composer back up the stairs, Pilsudski explained to Sandra that he was trying to find Ben McHugh. He was puzzled by her lack of reply until he followed her shocked gaze.

"Oh, don't worry about that. Just a test-run . . ." Pilsudski explained. "That's God Perkins."

Cavorting on Sandra's white chip gravel path was a terrifyingly ugly machine ridden by a soulful oily man in overalls. It emitted a brrrum brrrum with occasional backfires and bounced up and down on thick coil springs (the spare shock-absorbers from the Thorneycroft). The shape of the metal monster was that of a horse, its skull a huge piston-head welded on to a crankshaft and its tail a bundle of leaf-springs baled together. From the saddle roared great metallic cries and honkings.

"Where's Ben?" Joan Earth demanded as she sorted herself out after her confrontation with her new friend. "Have you got him upstairs?"

"Bring him out!" Fred shouted from his bucking steed. "Come on, Ben, I've done you proud. This will go down like a bomb. They'll love it. Once I've got a second silencer on we'll be away, no problems."

The different guests crowded in the hallway, obvious relief on their faces. At last the normal people had arrived.

"Hooray," shouted the chief biologist, hugging Harriet whom he had brought along, "let's give a big hand to the guests of honour."

Sandra stared miserably at God Perkins which was pissing oil on her blanched gravel.

"I would love to believe that you are all hallucinations," she said faintly. "There's no *need* for you to exist, is there?"

"Will Ben be back later? Has he left already?" Pilsudski insisted. "It's very important . . ."

Sandra stood aside as Fred rode God Perkins up the steps of her lakeside mansion and through the door, his oily fingers poised on the throttle. The clutch of the *deus ex machina* was in the right stirrup on a short spring. Gear was changed by the rider leaning heavily to one side. Changing up into second Fred urged his mount through the hallway and into the drawing-room.

"See that, Missus? Never even scuffed up the sheepskin rug at the door."

"That's remarkable," Sandra murmured with a lost smile, "but wouldn't you like to walk it over to the fireplace tiles and crack them? Or jump it through the window. Go ahead. I don't mind. There's a cabinet in the corner with some indifferent jade and porcelain that belonged to my father. Break it if you're in the mood. Ben would want you to feel at home."

Pilsudski sat down on the Chesterfield, patting the smoking rear-quarters of God Perkins.

"We need a sacrifice scene for the new play. Has Ben told you about it? Our composer—you've met him, he was here a minute ago—has written this altar music, you know, priests and chanting, oh it was years ago wasn't it, Stack?"

"Must have been 1964 when he composed it," the front-of-house manager confirmed. "It was streets ahead of its time."

"And it's scored for mouth-organ, jew's-harp, bongo-drums and clarinet which works out bonza. We've got actors in the company conversant with all those instruments. It's a stroke of luck. What's it called, Stack?"

"The Golden Calf."

"Graven images, the old robes swishing, and this weird music . . . we can't go wrong. The Poms will really get stirred up."

Sandra ignored Pilsudski and watched her normal guests who were admiring God Perkins and asking Fred technical questions about his mount. She wished that her baby Steiner would explode and decapitate them all with flying strings. When Frank Williams re-appeared at the door. his usual healthy colour regained and tottered across to the unco-operative piano, Sandra's vision of massacre seemed realizable. Here was a man who could trigger off destructive devices. She closed her eyes.

"Ever heard of Dionysius? This is my pre-Christian phase. It will fit into anything. The last time I used it was for the state opening of the biggest dry-dock in British Columbia. Jeeesus, it fitted in with the tide, the crowd, the scream of gulls . . ."

Jules Stack's hands smote the keyboard.

The sacrifice was made.

All the different guests relaxed, gratified by the presence of the mechanical horse and the phenomenally abnormal music that was dinning their ears. As the ex-composer fought his way through barrier after barrier of discord, Harriet disengaged herself from the Chief Biologist and stood by the Steiner, one elbow on the polished surface. It had been her practical, helpful instinct to clear up the mess made by Jules and now, moved to the depths of her sensible, womanly soul by the Chopinesque figure that coughed and sighed through its own barrage of sound, she fell in love.

As McHugh walked down the drive of Sandra's lakeside mansion, his travel-riter in one hand and his brown envelope of typescript in the other, Joan Earth jumped out of the bushes and wrapped her arms round his neck.

"There you are! Have you written my part yet? Come on, have me. Take me. I want you. Are there *lots of lines*? Here love, fold up my jumper . . . see how the sparks fly when I pull it over my hair? . . . put it under one elbow and stick my jeans under the other, then the gravel won't hurt your funny-bones. Christ Ben, I adore you . . ."

"Joan, Joan," McHugh sighed reproachfully, "don't sell yourself so cheap. All this for a few words? That's all I'm worth, a few words. Count the cost. Stand up straight, stick up for yourself and your craft as an actress."

Joan Earth sank McHugh's soul with a huge French kiss.

"Mmmm, words, words, I love your words . . . come on, your lady of the manor hasn't cut the grass for a long time. Let's have a frolic down there by the sundial. Don't forget to tell Peter which part I'm to have."

"Joan, the casting is Peter's prerogative . . ."

McHugh lifted up his head as he heard a monstrous crash from inside Sandra's lakeside mansion. It was repeated. Then it became a loud monotonous thud, the sound of a pile-driver. A piano, played with a disaster-headed *fortissimo*, struck up in accompaniment. McHugh ran down to the window of the drawing-room and looked inside. He saw his new character, God Perkins, dancing to the rhythms of a hound-faced man who was hammering the keys of the Steiner baby grand with a manic passion. As he watched, Fred switched on the amplifier under the saddle-horn of the mechanical horse and it began to sing. Sandra was sitting by herself in a corner, staring at the wall. McHugh noticed that she did not alter her sorrowful, haunted gaze, even when God Perkins reared up, perfectly controlled, bellowing out the last lines of "Linden Lea", and smashed its front hooves straight through the floorboards. The different guests laughed uncontrollably.

"Christ," McHugh breathed, "it works! It works! But who's that playing the piano so badly?"

"That's Weldon's brother," Joan Earth said disparagingly. "He's doing the music. Can you believe it? He's got a hand like a housebrick. Now, tell me about this part. Is it St Paul's wife?"

Fred backed God Perkins out of the hole which it had made in Sandra's floor, made the mechanical horse do a controlled rear, then cantered it to the door. As soon as there was enough space, he changed up through second to third and fourth, then galloped off up the drive, whooping and shouting, Pilsudski running by his stirrup, all the guests calling farewell over the roar of the diesel engine.


## nine · Meetings

Lionel Handlegrave toyed with an ivory paper-knife, pretending to read the quotations from the Koran which were scored on the haft. He was struggling to maintain a cool and steady exterior as he listened to the report of two of his network of drama officers who had unearthed a hideous conspiracy in the north-west of England, an area susceptible to attack and influence from Catholic Ireland and Mammonite America.

"You're quite sure he's *nouveau riche?*" he inquired, as lightly as he could.

"Well sir, we've done some checking this morning with his ex-employers. His address used to be a private housing estate in a district of Liverpool where house-prices have trebled in three years. He was definitely a Rotarian and a Freemason. We have it on good authority that he played golf—not on municipal courses either . . . it all looks pretty damning."

Lionel Handlegrave sighed and looked out of the window.

"How can a man like that have the gall to apply for a bursary, never mind trying to take over one of our theatres? He must be unbalanced or completely out of touch."

"Glenda thinks that he's spearheading a general take-over bid by the new middle class, aided by Pilsudski who comes from a suburb of Melbourne. I must say it looks fairly sinister. Neither of them have ever *suffered*, nor felt the brunt of the capitalist jackboot. Pilsudski has all the colonial attitudes, go-getting, sweeping sensitivity aside, general iconoclasm . . ."

"All right, all right!" Lionel Handlegrave murmured, holding up a beautifully manicured hand and showing two inches of thick blue and white stripe starched linen cuff. "But we have to prove it. I can't go to the committee without concrete evidence."

Dearden Ryan looked uncomfortable.

"Sir, we have to be honest about this. We're in a bit of a jam. We think the situation up there may be much more complicated. Geoffrey and I were discussing it late last night and we decided that the only parallel we could draw was between the Anarchists and Communists when they started fighting each other in Barcelona during the Spanish Civil War, leaving the Republican cause discredited . . ."

"Oh, indeed?" Lionel Handlegrave arched his sleek eyebrows.

"You see, sir, we're not absolutely certain of Glenda Stand-Crashaw."

Lionel Handlegrave frowned. As Senior Drama Administrator he had to deal with labyrinthine human problems, trying to make a cohesive and culturally acceptable pattern out of chaos. One thing that always came to his aid was his instinct. He had personally vetted Glenda Stand-Crashaw on the occasion of her promotion from box-office girl to assistant manager. He had not found any social weakness in her background, or any chink into which a lever could be forced by an unprincipled agency. She was rock solid, exactly the kind of material needed to keep theatre on the right course.

He adopted a slight lifting of the upper lip.

"You know her aunt . . ."

"Yes, sir," Geoffrey admitted hurriedly. "Wonderful organizer. First-rate. I saw her in action during a visit to Brixton

Youth Theatre. She actually played leapfrog with a group of Jamaican reformed junkies. Terrific stuff."

Lionel Handlegrave pointed at Geoffrey Block with his ivory paper-knife. "You'd better know what you're doing. I've got Glenda earmarked for higher things. Are you going to prove me wrong?"

"It's only a doubt at this stage, sir. We could be completely haywire. Both of us feel rather badly about the whole business but we felt that we had to put it before you . . ." Dearden Ryan tailed off lamely, aware of the crystal sharpness of his superior's eye behind the plain-glass lenses of his gold-wire spectacles.

"You know that her great-grandfather was a working pipelayer on the first Lake District reservoir project? The old man was up there, waist-deep in the morass, monkeywrench in hand . . ." Lionel Handlegrave said darkly.

"Yes, sir, we know."

"Her mother worked in the Land Army, actually forking manure into barrows and *pushing* it . . ."

"Oh yes, sir, a favourite story of ours."

"*Story?*" Lionel Handlegrave snapped. "Are you doubting its authenticity? Good God, men, are you aware of just how few really genuine people there are working in theatre in Britain today? I can count them on one hand! When I find one I jump for joy! Look, it is my job to break up the pattern of insincerity in our theatrical life and replace those patterns with real values that have social significance. Glenda is from working-class stock! And you have the temerity to question her worth."

Geoffrey Block appealled to his colleague. He felt quite faint. His own after-shave, 'Groin', was mingling with Lionel Handlegrave's in a collision of perfumes which echoed the clash of their wills. He could not bear to see his superior hurt in this way.

"Please, Dearden . . . will you tell . . ."

Dearden Ryan took a deep breath. If his interpretation of the case was faulty then it was almost inevitable that the Senior Drama Administrator would transfer him to the vacant post of drama adviser to the Warrington Corporation. Outside the metropolis, Dearden Ryan would wither away and die.

"Sir, we just felt that we had to bring it to your notice. It seemed to us quite wrong to suppress the information, even though both of us admire Glenda and the way she copes with that theatre . . ."

Lionel Handlegrave closed his eyes.

"What has she done?" he said coldly. "That's all I want to know."

"It may be nothing, sir . . ." Dearden Ryan stammered. "You might put a different interpretation on the whole thing."

Geoffrey Block excused himself and went out into the corridor. Staggering to the end he pushed open the door of the toilet and managed to get to a basin before he was sick with fright. Glenda had *tenure*. Surely she was immovable! What had he been thinking of to join Dearden Ryan in this approach? Had Geoffrey Block gone mad? After three years of teaching art to the children of American diplomats, Geoffrey Block should have known better than to tamper with his rights to this present job. When Lionel threw them both out into the street, where would they go? It was a cold, cold world out there.

Lionel Handlegrave stared in disbelief at Dearden Ryan. His well-shaved jowl hung slack.

"Glenda?"

"Yes, sir."

"An engagement ring?"

"Round her neck, sir. She knew it was unacceptable. We weren't supposed to see it."

"How did you see it?"

Dearden Ryan paused and shrugged, showing more confidence than he was experiencing.

"We were doing an exercise in tactile expression, sir, establishing valid contact between separate bodies and sharing a common emotion. As you know, it's part of every progressive theatre's routine these days . . ."

"Good God, I'm amazed. Glenda! That deep into the bourgeoisie! Wearing a tawdry wealth-emblem like that. I think I'd have found it easier to forgive her if she'd flaunted it on her finger. You were quite right to bring it to my attention."

Dearden Ryan sighed with relief. The worst was over.

"It puts a new complexion on your visit. What we're dealing with is a full-scale infiltration up there, from two sides. I only hope that the Dramacart can survive being simultaneously attacked by the process of embourgeoisement and the *nouveau riche*. It will be a test of its standing with the working class. I want a full report in ten days. Get to it Dearden, and leave no stone unturned. Good luck."

McHugh walked back to the Dramacart site alongside God Perkins, listening to the rumbling voice that croaked and boomed from under the saddle. Joan Earth trotted behind, still asking about St Paul's wife. Ahead of the cavalcade strode Pilsudski, his bright ape-like face brilliant. This was going to be the breakthrough. This play. It would smash through all the old Pom conventions and rejuvenate the ailing English, turn them from their economic laments, their mindless football and shoddy materialism. God Perkins would stampede the Poms towards a new world where the sun shone and the air was clear. The great cultural outflow would be turned back to its source. An Australian would turn that great multi-coloured tide! Back across the Pacific and Atlantic would surge a current to wash the shores of Britain and make it live again. A new dynamism would be found. The Poms would work harder, with determination and grit. All the old over-civilized tiredness would vanish.

With a double backfire and a smell of burning rubber God Perkins fell to its knees, pitching Fred on to his head in the road.

"Christ, Fred, you could use that trick contrapuntally with the controlled rear," Pilsudski said delightedly, addressing his observation to the prostrate engineer. "Not sure about the smoking oil pouring from its nostrils though."

God Perkins groaned and fell on its side. Fred grumbled with disappointment.

McHugh folded his arms, looking at the mess.

"Peter, if we're going to keep *The Blinding Light* in the repertoire for six months then the mechanical horse will have to be more reliable than this. It's only covered a mile and the bloody thing is burnt out. Look at Fred, he's supposed to be the one who'll keep it going." McHugh prodded the inert engineer with his toe. "Not much expertise here, is there?"

"It'll be all right on the night, Ben. Don't worry," Pilsudski assured the worried writer. "This was only a test run."

Fred picked himself up off the road, fingering a graze on

c

his forehead. He studied the overturned machine and chewed his oily knuckles.

"No bother!" he gabbled. "No bother. It won't happen again. Don't cut my part. I can handle it. Front suspension went. I can take the strain off that link by building in two tensile torsion-bars and an anti-roll bar in the chest."

With the help of McHugh and Pilsudski, Bill righted God Perkins. Starting it up again he tinkered with the fuel pump, changed a filter, adjusted a screw in the right knee, put it into gear and led the horse by the rein at a snail's pace.

"Ben, you did promise me that St Paul would have a wife, or at least a girlfriend," Joan Earth whispered as she took McHugh's arm and jostled her projecting breast into his bicep. "Peter will make a terrific job of putting me into a direct sexual relationship with a saint."

"Not now, Joan," McHugh sighed. "I can't do two things at once. Peter wants this sacrifice scene. There's this musician to contend with. Look, St Paul didn't like women. He said you should only get married if you have to. I can't alter his fundamental prejudices."

"Plenty of men don't like women, but they get married. I don't have to have any actual scenes with St Paul. Couldn't I have a lover? What about a Roman lover, in armour? Wardrobe have got all the *Julius Caesar* costumes from last year . . ."

McHugh broke his stride and crossed to the other side of the road. He had a lot on his mind. The sacrifice scene was definitely Old Testament. It had no place in a story based on the Acts of the Apostles. He would have to have a show-down with Pilsudski about this type of interference. It was bending the centre of the play, forcing it off at a tangent. Either a writer had integrity or he died. Pilsudski would have to be put in his place.

"When did the Virgin Mary die, Ben?" Joan Earth asked from his elbow.

"Please, Joan, not now . . ."

"Didn't Jesus Christ have any grandchildren? A grand-daughter? Couldn't I be her? A long-lost granddaughter? Don't you like my performance in *The Unfathomable Grass*? Have I ever let you down?"

McHugh broke into a trot to escape from the insistent actress. She followed him, her nubile shape vibrating through the night, still breathing suggestions. When McHugh reached his caravan he found Lulu peering through a crack in the curtains at Beryl and the police sergeant who were trying to define obscenity.

"Stay with me tonight," Joan Earth panted. "We can get this new part sorted out. Couldn't God Perkins have a Greek goddess as an assistant? Wasn't a lot of early Christian practice just an adaptation of old Greek mythology? Don't you think I'd make a good Aphrodite?"

Beryl's Raleigh bicycle was parked against the side of the caravan. For once, demoralized after the failure of the Normality party, she had left it unlocked. McHugh seized it, mounted, and pedalled off into the night, leaving Joan Earth in the shadows.

"Rotten sod!" the actress hissed, tossing back her black mane.

"Bloody fool!" yelled Beryl at the height of her revenge with Authority.

"Opportunist!" ground Sean as he narrowly missed the unilluminated cyclist on his return in the Volkswagen from visiting Ed on the island and making the arrangements for the private performance of *Dream*.

It was a long uphill ride to Harriet's flat. As McHugh heaved down on the pedals he wrestled mentally with Pilsudski. It was as if he was faced with the problem of pinning down a flame. Pilsudski would merely flow round his objections and keep his ideas burning. Much as he loved the man's pure energy, his daring deviousness worried McHugh. It meant that the writer was always doomed to lose. Take this matter of the sacrifice scene and the composer. Instead of being forced to compose music for the play *after* it had been written, the terrible pianist was being afforded the privilege of having old work slotted in. How could the play survive this kind of grafting operation? Those notes came from an icebound Canadian winter, not the warm climes of the eastern Mediterranean. All right. The composer was notorious for his inability to meet deadlines. That was a pity. The composer had problems. He sparked off on different stimuli from McHugh. But why should he be allowed to use the natural compassion of other artistic souls to his own benefit while McHugh's play, written white-hot in a day and half a night in a slate-quarry, got knocked about and partially demolished? The *feel* of the Old Testament was contrary to that of the Acts. It was another sensation altogether, the jealous god, not the god of love. McHugh decided to refuse the sacrifice scene, and the music which went with it. The composer would have to buckle down and work from the script, fitting his music to the mood and action.

McHugh leant the bicycle up against the wall at the bottom of the iron stairs leading to Harriet's flat, and went up. He was glad to see that the light was on. Harriet was probably revising for her examinations. Opening the door with his key, McHugh was surprised and disappointed to find the terrible pianist sitting at the table surrounded by empty dishes, glasses and bottles, smoking a cigarette in a holder. Curled up on the settee was Harriet. From her expression it was obvious that she had not expected the writer and would have preferred it if he had not come.

"Oh," was all McHugh could manage, "sorry."

The hound-faced man stood up, steadied himself on a silver-topped stick, and thrust out a hand.

"How nice."

McHugh took the hand, lost for a rejoinder. From behind thick pebble lenses he caught an amused and unsober leer.

"Ben, this is Jules Stack," Harriet said curtly.

"Weldon's brother?" McHugh queried. "The composer?"

"Ex-composer."

"But you've come to do the music . . ."

"No, I've come to stick old music into a new play. It's just lying around doing nothing. I think I've finished with music. How much National Assistance would I get if I decided to stay here?"

"Jules, Ben is the person who's written the play," Harriet steered the ebullient ex-composer back to the table and poured the last of her Beaujolais Villages into his carved green-slate goblet. Jules smiled up at McHugh.

"You're mad. Come on the National Assistance with me. Don't try and fight it, son. They'll beat you into the ground. Do you know, I'm the only serious artist ever to be thrown out of the Columbia Chamber Orchestra concert hall still with the baton in his hand? What's the point of struggling on? They can never find you a job as a writer. Register as a writer. Ah, they might send for underwriter, or shipwrighter.

Put 'author'. How many jobs do you see advertised for 'author'? None. Come on the National Assistance. Isn't this girl beautiful? She's beautiful."

"Harriet, may I have a word with you?" McHugh said quietly.

"No, Ben. Where words are concerned you can keep your distance."

"I've got nowhere to sleep."

Harriet looked across at Jules who was prodding a hand-painted porcelain egg around the tablecloth with the rubber end of his stick and shouting 'goal'.

"Ben, I feel I can help him. Do you understand that? With you it's futile. You don't need help. You need locking up. But with him—how can I put it?—there's a *need* . . ."

"Will you let me sleep on the sofa?"

"You don't want to sleep with me?"

"I thought you wanted to help Beethoven here."

"Oho, I heard that!" Jules Stack roared, a paranoid brightness arriving in his bloodshot eyes. "Roll over Beethoven!"

With a crash of breaking green-slate goblet Jules Stack fell forward on to the table, scattering glass and crockery. A deep-seated instinct for self-preservation and many years of practice in the bars of Ottawa had provided the ex-composer with an automatic system of self-defence on such occasions. His silver-topped stick was drawn up into his chest, one hand shot rigidly to the pocket containing his Canadian Social Security card and covered it, his knees cracked together, and his glasses eased up over his forehead. Only the inanimate suffered fracture and disruption. Life, Jules Stack, was safe, even in escape.

"Poor lamb," Harriet crooned soothingly as she cleared the broken goblet away from the area of his head. "He must be exhausted."


## ten · Gemini

McHugh suppressed any outward signs of his humiliation as he helped Harriet to carry the comatose ex-composer through to the bedroom and lay him out on the light-blue continental quilt which was embroidered with bright red beavers building a dam in a backwater. There was an uncomfortable pause as McHugh stood at the end of the bed, Jules Stack's zip-up boots in his hands, the silver-topped walking stick under his arm.

"I suppose you want me to leave now?" he said. "I'll push off."

"Aren't you going to sleep on the sofa?" Harriet grinned archly.

"Where are you going to sleep?"

"I think I'll go round to mother's."

"Won't she find that rather odd?"

"Not when I tell her that I'm taking refuge from you. Mother thought your play was fascinating, Ben, but she's of the opinion that you would be better off in London where the mentally unstable are automatically afforded pre-eminence and respect. She thinks that if you get into television you might have a chance of salvation. Within three years you'd be screaming to get out and into the real world. Then you could come back up here and work for the Forestry Commission or one of the boat-hire businesses."

McHugh sat on the end of the bed, eyeing the feet of the terrible pianist. Was this the ultimate fate of the artist? The holes, the frayed bottoms of his corduroy trousers? The glottal snore of an entranced soul? Did he want to end up like this dreaming escapee? The ravaged landscape of Jules Stack was a tragic sight, an outline of the blitz after flights of black bombers from purgatory had raided the human psyche. What was he looking for? Did *The Blinding Light have* to be produced at all? Wouldn't the world keep turning without God Perkins? Where was it all leading? To this? Derelict, defiant, doped Jules Stack? Could McHugh take such a fall? Could he steadfastly look this kind of bleak future in the eye? Beryl had repeatedly told him that a self-employed person, even if he religiously bought his stamps, could never draw unemployment pay, or sick pay. He was *outside*. He was presumed to have no social needs, having sought out strange anti-social freedoms of his own. In ten years McHugh might be forced to lay his large frame down in bus shelters, under bushes, or in Salvation Army hostels, an outcast. Self-expression could ruin as well as reward. Did he really have talent? Was it recognizable? Was it the kind of talent that ordinary people *liked*?

"I'll see you in the morning. Will you make his breakfast if I don't get round in time? He likes proper coffee and thick toast with plenty of butter and maybe a glass or two of cider afterwards."

McHugh nodded dully.

Carefully Harriet drew her pyjamas from under the pillow and slipped from the room on tip-toe. McHugh heard the door close behind her.

"Has she gone?"

McHugh turned sharply, encountering the bleary eyes of Jules Stack who had partially raised his head from the pillow.

"Well, has she?" The Lazarus-like figure demanded.

"Yes," McHugh managed to reply, taken aback by the resurrection.

"Thank Christ for that. I'd never have made it, not tonight. Had to play possum. What does she keep in the fridge? Know where everything is? When you're tired, do you find it difficult to respond? Let's talk about this play. Jeeezus, I can't stand that bastard Beardsley. Did you ever see a woman like that? Here, pass that china milkmaid over. There's no ash-tray. Do you smoke?"

A numbing lethargy gripped McHugh as he groped for the china ornament. One minute he was facing a drunken wreck, a leaking ship flung against the rocks, the next minute he was being interrogated by a weird, battered puck of a man blowing smoke-rings at the straw manikins on the bedside table. How?

"Do you want something to eat?" he found himself saying. "A bowl of soup maybe? Cheese on toast?"

Jules Stack swung his feet off the bed and wriggled his toes into his boots. To McHugh those feet were now magical. The winged feet of a Mercury.

"Later. We've got other things to talk about. Let's get this sacrifice scene sorted out. Harriet's got her uncle's piano-accordion somewhere, so she said. We can use that in place of something better. Make some coffee. We can have this wrapped up by morning then you can show me round this dump. My little brother is busy calculating how many people walk out during your current play. He's done some analyses, so he says. He reckons that, *pro rata*, more people have walked out of your play than have ever walked in. Is that possible? Have you ever read Mordecai Richler? You should."

McHugh followed the ex-composer into the living-room and obediently lit the gas-fire, when instructed to do so. Jules Stack fitted his cigarette into his holder and lay back in an easy chair.

"Now, the opening will need to be strong. It starts off with a triumphal march which we'll score for five jew's harps instead of the two I've presently got down. Any bastard, even a lame-brain actor, can play the jew's harp. Root around for that squeeze-box after you've ground the coffee and I'll play it for you. I thought some kind of chant, repetitive. Ever actually seen a human sacrifice? What the hell do you think *I* am?"

McHugh stared at the wall as he pressed the button on the Moulinex electric grinder. Under the impress of the ex-composer's dominant personality and his natural assumption of power in their working relationship, McHugh had forgotten to put the plastic cover on the machine. The coffee-beans shot from the chamber like pellets from a scatter-gun, rattling against the kitchen walls and stinging McHugh's face.

"What's going on in there?" Jules Stack shouted. "Are you playing the Chinese Blocks? I never scored any goddamned Chinese Blocks! Bring the squeeze-box for Chrissake!"

McHugh took his hands away from his eyes and poured a fresh supply of beans into the chamber. Far down in his slow-working nature a bubble of resentment was being formed. By the time that he had made the coffee and found the piano-accordion, this bubble had risen perilously close to the surface.

Jules Stack tasted the coffee and spat it back into the cup.

"Yargh! When will you bastards learn to make decent coffee over here? This is shit man! Make some more! Pom-da-da-pom-pom-pom-pom . . . here's the opening phrase . . ."

McHugh did not return to the kitchen. He sipped his own coffee and kept looking at the artificial flames in the gas fire. All his life he had hated himself whenever he had lost his temper. It made him ashamed. The strength which he admired above all others was the strength of the creative mind, the strength of the builder. Beryl had often taunted him to the precipice of violence, but McHugh had walked away. Once he had struck her. The shame had been agonizing. The accusation of being a bully had crippled him with self-doubt.

Was he? Had he not bullied her out of one life into another? McHugh followed the flames and tried to ignore the stream of instructions from the hound-faced persecutor who was now playing the piano-accordion, terribly.

"La-la, pom-pom . . . see? It needs to be emphatic, regal. No one will hear the goddamned words anyway. You can never hear words on stage. I don't know why they don't make do with some kind of musical phonetics. It's the music that matters. How about a fried egg? I'm just in the mood for a fried egg."

McHugh stood up. Putting a hand on each end of the piano-accordion he pressed it shut. When the last wail had left the instrument he pulled it away from the ex-composer's shoulders, half taking him out of his seat.

"Keeerist, be careful! You'll knot my lungs!" Jules Stack croaked. "I'm a chronic asthmatic!"

"If you keep trying to stuff your old music into my new play I'll plait your prick to your tie and play hoop with your arsehole," McHugh said.

Jules Stack blinked worriedly, biting on his cigarette-holder.

"Jeeeezus, you're paranoid! You've got a problem man. We're supposed to be working together. How can I write music for a man's words if he's antagonistic towards me? You've despised me from the first moment we met. Why do you look down on me? Come on, let's have it. You're envious. Music is the most immediate of the arts, right? All you scribblers aspire to the condition of the composer. I put together a superb piece of dramatic music and you say no. Just like that. You're crazy. It fits exactly. It's biblical, for Chrissake. It *sounds* right. One minute I'm asked to write music for a mechanical horse and the next you're turning down the simplest and most acceptable tunes I offer. Give a little. Boy, you're so rigid. The days of the artistic autocrat are over. Get this, I've been in this business a long time. I'm an ex-composer. So how can you screw me up like this when my stuff *fits*. There's no other way we can work. You have to have the sacrifice scene, and my theme music for Canadian Navy helicopters on coastal patrol. It's what *exists*. Come on now, bend a little."

McHugh smiled grimly, one hand on the door-knob.

"Any Christmas carols you want slotted in?"

"There's a string quartet called 'The Rocky Mountains Hydro-Electric Scheme in D Minor' I thought we might use for the River Jordan baptism scene."

"There is no River Jordan baptism scene."

"I thought this goddamned play was supposed to be biblical. How can you be biblical and leave out the River Jordan?"

"How can you be a composer and not write music?"

"I keep telling you, I'm an ex-composer. An ex-composer *has written* music. You and I will represent a fusion of past and present. Do you like T. S. Eliot?"

McHugh opened the door and made the most purposeful exit he could. Jumping on Beryl's bicycle he pedalled off through the night in search of Pilsudski and Weldon Stack. As he rode down the hill towards Borrans Field and the sleeping theatre he saw nothing but critical times ahead.

The following morning a deputation from the Orrestwater Council arrived at the Dramacart to see the co-general managers. Mr Thomas accompanied them, armed with rolls of ticker-tape from a computer. Sean Kel showed the deputation into his purple caravan and offered them Indian or Chinese tea and an assortment of Hebridean biscuits while Glenda put a selection of well-loved fox-hunting songs on the hi-fi. Five minutes later, the police sergeant arrived in a panda car and joined the party. Pilsudski was in rehearsal, having spent most of the night persuading McHugh to give Jules Stack another chance to prove himself. Time was now of the essence. The artistic director had few clear working days to put the show together before opening night. When Weldon Stack reported the arrival of the deputation and the police sergeant, Pilsudski took little notice. He was busy establishing the character of the early St Paul, the persecutor of the early Christians, the Nazi of the Syrian seaboard.

"I think it means trouble," Weldon Stack advised Pilsudski. "They're probably making the initial approach to get *The Unfathomable Grass* banned."

"What?" Pilsudski asked, screwing up his eyes. "What's that?"

"Ben's play."

"Oh, you mean Ben's *other* play."

"The one in the repertoire."

"Ah, yes. Well that's not my problem. Could you ask

around to see if anyone's got a portable furnace we could use?"

"A portable furnace? What for?"

"The torture scene. Heating the tongs and pincers."

"That's the stage-manager's job."

"Aren't you the stage-manager?"

"No, I'm the front-of-house manager, your friend, Weldon Stack."

"Ah."

Pilsudski turned back to his actors. He could see it all. Joan Earth hanging on the wall in chains. Murphy Winspear stripped to the waist, about to brand an innocent and resolute virgin with the symbol of the fish. Even the stink of scorching flesh would be there, pumped out of a Belling one-plate electric stove where belly pork was grilling at regulo 6. Stage-management were already on to it.

"Mr Kel . . ." began the chief executive officer, "you know we have no watch committee here. Up until now it has not been found necessary. However, there are councillors who have been putting pressure on us to form one in order to deal with the question of this play, *The Unfathomable Grass*."

"Oh yes," Sean nodded, "the play all the fuss is about."

"You acknowledge that there is a fuss?" A lady councillor who ran two gift shops and a riding stable chimed in. "Then why don't you take the wretched thing off?"

Sean smiled agreeably.

"These issues are a little more complex that that," he said soothingly. "As you know, there is no official censorship now that the Lord Chamberlain's office has been abolished."

"We're not concerned with what's official!" the lady councillor scolded. "We just want that filth taken off."

"Could we have it in writing?" Glenda said as she settled down on her camel-skin pouffe, flexing her left hand so the councillors could admire her new finger ornament as the light played on the considerable jewels. "That would help. You see, we're not responsible for the artistic direction of the theatre. We are the business managers only."

"Who is responsible then?"

"The artistic director."

"Then we'll see him."

"He's in rehearsal at the moment."

"Well, get him out."

"We can't do that."

"Why not?"

"He's rehearsing a new play to go into the repertoire."

"So you are taking *The Unfathomable Grass* off?"

Glenda shook her head.

"No, he's *not* putting the new play in to replace the one which you find so offensive. Actually, the new work is by *the same author.*"

Glenda dipped into her teacup as the bombshell exploded. Sean adopted an expression of grave concern, waiting for the fury of the councillors to subside.

"Just hold on a minute," the police sergeant butted in before Sean could deliver his mollifying words. "Hang on a second. No one has *proved* that this play is obscene in the proper letter of the Law. I mean, Janet, do you really know what's obscene?"

"Indeed I do! Oh yes! And I don't need you to tell me what's filth and what isn't. We've all heard about your latest affair, sergeant, terrible! Striking up with *his* wife! Why don't you stick to your job? You could stop those youths spraying slogans all over my display windows for a start. You're going off the rails, do you know that? Right off!" the lady councillor blared.

The police sergeant reddened and clutched his helmet to his chest, silent.

"All right, Mr Kel. We've known you for a few years. Before, you've brought us plays we liked. I remember your production of *Hay Fever* with affection and admiration. Tell us what's going on. Put us in the picture. We can see from the outside that something's gone wrong. Now don't worry about us thinking that you're talking behind people's backs. This is a practical problem we're facing. We've heard whispers of the trouble you're having with the other side. We're not as daft as we seem sometimes. Good Lord, when I think of the trouble we have with the councillors sometimes, at each other's throats, splitting up into factions . . ."

Sean acknowledged the chief executive's understanding with a reserved smile.

"Well, I have to admit we do have . . . shall we say, a difference of opinion with the artistic director . . ."

"We have a right to our likes and dislikes as well," Glenda pointed out reasonably. "We are individuals."

"Do you like this play?" The lady councillor asked openly. "Do you, as two decent people, like this play?"

Glenda looked at the floor, a curious smile of discomfort on her fresh full lips.

"Enough said!" The lady councillor said triumphantly. "Enough said."

Sean held up a hand.

"Please, bear with us. Give us some time. What we have to think of is the future. Do you honestly think that we want to alienate our Orrestwater audience? What we want is a situation whereby we'll be welcome every year. As you said, sir, when I think of the people who came to see *Hay Fever*, *She Stoops To Conquer*, oh all the good stuff we've done in the past, I can see what *must be done*. But we are not in complete control."

"But how long will it take?" The lady councillor insisted. "One of my nieces has seen it four times already. She's given up her nursing training and gone to join a commune. Poor Betty's going mad with worry."

"Somehow or other," Sean declared grimly, "we will resolve this situation within the next week. The Dramacart Moving Theatre will return to being the loved and respected institution that it used to be."

The chief executive thought for a moment, then raised a quizzical eyebrow at the power behind his authority, the lady councillor.

"That all right?"

"Seven days. But after that we must act if nothing has happened. It must come off one way or the other."

The caravan heaved on its springs as the deputation stood up in preparation for moving off.

## eleven · A letter received by the General Manager (Ex Acting Co-General Manager) on the Monday morning, upsetting his consortium

501 Beaufort Street
London W1

Dear Sean Kel,

How nice to hear from you. Very interested in your plan for Glenda's development. You know how I share your belief in her enormous potential as an arts officer, helping to design and shape our national identity through cultural forces. She is the kind of individual one cannot help admiring, such is her high level of integrity and the *energy*, the sheer energy that lies at the bottom of her personality. If you asked me to name a person better qualified to be co-general manager of the Dramacart, I would have to admit defeat. Glenda is a truly dedicated cultural administrator and will inevitably rise through the hierarchy. One day I would not be surprised to find her next door, sharing this corridor. Wonderful girl. However I think it might be a tiny bit previous to bump her up to co-general manager at this stage. I think a few months longer in the job of assistant manager (she has three months service in that position anyway), would do her a world of good and make my position stronger when I eventually approach the Theatrefund Central Committee.

Dearden and Geoffrey are catching the 11.30 a.m. train tomorrow and ask if you might meet them. They have things to talk about which might be better discussed away from the theatre environs. As you know, Sean, we are in the middle of an unsettled period right now. feeling the repercussions of the Depression. There are forces at work within the theatre that are negative, trying to use it for self-aggrandizement and to achieve political change in favour of the more privileged classes.

Please stop paying Glenda her acting allowance as co-general manager. She should start at the basic rate anyway.

Great news about your engagement. Hope you'll be very happy together, both you dear people.

Yours ever,

LIONEL HANDLEGRAVE

P.S. Could you tell me where Ben McHugh was educated and whether he played Rugby Union or Rugby League?

## twelve · Human Sacrifice

McHugh could hardly keep his eyes open. All night, all morning, and now half way through the afternoon, he had argued with Pilsudski, refusing to write in a sacrifice scene for Jules Stack's piece, 'The Golden Calf'. He had even resorted to scripture itself to prove that when Moses discovered Aaron and the Children of Israel worshipping the bovine effigy, he had not actually caught them sacrificing human victims to it. Pilsudski was not impressed with this display of lame erudition. He knew that the Children of Israel *would have liked* to offer up human sacrifices on this occasion. Then there was Time: centuries separated the incident on the road to Damascus from the action central to 'The Golden Calf'. But Time was bendable, Pilsudski insisted. As long as it was used as a legitimate illustration, the Stone Age and 1984 could be placed in conjunction with one another with telling effect. What they were working in was *theatre*, the most fluid and flexible treatment of truth ever devised. *The Blinding Light* would be the enactment of a mystery and, as such, had all the licence needed to transform god into devil, heaven into hell, or horse into diesel engine. What was a human sacrifice beside this awesome amalgam of changes?

McHugh sat in the back row, glaring morosely at the stage. With the set for *The Unfathomable Grass* still up, Pilsudski was plotting the moves for the opening scene in the torture chamber. Joan Earth, still brooding over McHugh's refusal to create for her a major role as St Paul's wife, was pretending to improvise jolts of agony through her torso as Murphy Winspear jabbed at her with a red strip of plywood. But Joan Earth's heart was not in her work. Today her career was an unhappy sham. She longed to be in Fulham or queueing up to audition for a bacon commercial. She had been betrayed.

"Come on, Joan," Pilsudski chided her. "Have you ever been in great pain?"

"I'm in great pain now," she answered darkly, sliding down from her pose against the fireplace into an armchair. "You know damn well what's upset me."

"I don't, Joan," Pilsudski murmured. "Come to Daddy."

"Oh shut up!"

"Come on, let's hear it," Pilsudski said comfortingly as he vaulted on to the stage and sat on the arm of the chair. "What's screwing you up?"

"Oh I feel so trapped!" Joan Earth burst out in a flood of

tears. "So trapped. I should be down in London. My agent said I could walk into a part in a new tour of *Oh Calcutta* which is going to Moscow, but I'm stuck up here . . ."

"You're being unfair, Joan. We can't dictate to Ben who he puts in his plays. A writer has to have integrity."

"I know all about Ben's integrity," Joan Earth hissed. "I've had as much integrity with that lying sod as most. He doesn't stick to his word."

Under the accusing eyes of the rest of the company, McHugh got up and left the auditorium. As he walked down the wooden steps to ground level, Harriet drove up in her Fiat 124. Sitting next to her was the ex-composer.

"Are we all set to go? Did they get the extra jew's harps?" he shouted as he got out, a sheaf of mutilated papers under his arm. "Did I hear the director say it was a clarinet or was it a flute? I prefer the flute. Or even a flageolet."

Weldon Stack left his caravan and a breakfast of Java Old Government black coffee and croissants to greet his brother. As they said good morning, Pilsudski told the company to take a ten-minute break while he talked Joan Earth out of breaking her contract. They scattered from the huge tin box into the sun, Fiona McPhee, tall, dark-haired, weightily graceful as an antelope, running in the fore, her Gaelic eyes upturned and blue as the summer sky.

Jules Stack put his stick through her legs, bringing her crashing to the ground, then threw himself on top of her.

"Have you seen Joan?" Weldon Stack asked Murphy Winspear as they hauled the plunging ex-composer off his prey. "I think she can give me a helping hand here. Would you ask her to step over?"

"She's with Peter. There's a bit of a hassle on at the moment. Joan's throwing one of her tantrums."

The winded actress staggered to her feet, glaring furiously at a bemused Jules Stack who feinted at her with his stick again, chuckling warmly.

"Say, you've got quite a colour. I like a woman with rosy cheeks."

"Are you some kind of fucking madman?" she snarled.

"No, no, it's the way you run. Like a gazelle. Keeerist, I haven't seen anything so exotic since I saw the Harlem Globetrotters. What's your name?"

Fiona McPhee rubbed her shins.

"Are you taking the mick out of me?"

"I could find you a piece I wrote a few years back that would suit you to a T. What was it called now . . . yeh, *The Flight Of The Caribou To The Tundra*. I'll play it for you."

Fiona McPhee smiled delightedly.

"Will you really?"

Harriet touched her mouth with a thoughtful finger and quietly said good-bye to Jules Stack, getting back into her Fiat 124. She had never met a man with such charm.

Sean Kel and Glenda Stand-Crashaw had witnessed the scene through the Moorish arch of the box-office. Sean had been glad of the diversion. Since he had shown Lionel Handle-grave's letter to his consort, she had not spoken a word.

"He seems an interesting character. Very distinguished-looking isn't he? Weldon seems very fond of him. He's paying the fee for the music himself, but we're not to mention that. I wish I had a brother like that . . ." Sean meandered on, struggling to fill the awful silences. "Glenda, please . . . it's not my fault. I did my best."

Glenda folded her arms and pressed her lips even tighter together. Beneath her Shetland knitwear there was no tell-tale bump. The engagement-ring lay on the floor where she had thrown it in a fit of petulant fury.

"When Dearden and Geoffrey get up here, we'll sort things out. Don't worry about it. Pilsudski and McHugh will hang themselves, given enough rope. Everything is going for us. Now Beryl is on our side and has instructed a solicitor to take out a private injunction against McHugh to get *The Unfathomable Grass* banned, we can't lose. She says if that fails she'll go to the Home Office and then to the House of Lords."

Glenda strode across the box-office, twisted the top off a bottle of blue-black ink and poured it all over Sean's paper-work.

McHugh drove down to Sandra's lakeside mansion in his Midget. Fred had not yet repaired the silencer, all his time being devoted to the welfare of God Perkins and persuading the Equity deputy to support his application for membership of the actors' union. The writer was unconcerned with the monstrous farting of his vehicle as it wound through Orrest-water. He did not care what happened to him. Weldon Stack had often told him that all writers were paranoid—that this mental condition was one of the basic qualifications for the job—but McHugh felt that right now he *was* being perse-cuted. All his friends had deserted, or betrayed him. Only that morning Beryl had delivered, by hand, a solicitor's letter giving him notice of her intention to sue him for both obscenity and divorce, and then gone off to school on her bicycle. Weldon Stack, his trusted friend, had broken faith by peaching on his whereabouts. Pilsudski . . . well, Pilsudski was selling out to an ex-composer whom he hardly knew and an engineer with a fatal disease of the ego. Sean and Glenda were out to destroy him. Harriet had deserted him. There was only Sandra.

Sandra was sitting in her oak-panelled living-room which overlooked the broad, still lake, watching two joiners re-lay her floor. In the hall was a pile of luggage. Dark shadows lay under her sharp, dark eyes, and her voice was shaky and fatigued as she briefly asked Ben to go away and never come back again. That afternoon she was catching a plane to the Canary Islands.

"Be fair, Sandra . . ." McHugh said in a low voice, em-barrassed by the presence of the two craftsmen who were listening attentively. "It wasn't my fault."

"This man is the person responsible for bringing the mech-anical horse I told you about into my house," Sandra ex-plained to them, a cigarette in her trembling fingers. "You say you don't believe me. Why don't you ask him?"

"All right, lady. Did you bring a mechanical horse in here?" one of the joiners asked, a smile on his hardened face. "Or should I ask first: does this mechanical horse exist or is the lady here one of these wealthy eccentrics?"

McHugh looked at the jagged crater in the floor and the new timbers stacked by the Steiner baby grand. Again, he heard that dreadful music.

"I suppose it's true. Look, it's a prop in a play I've written. That's all. A piece of theatrical make-believe. A symbol if you like. Sandra love, can't we talk? How about some coffee?"

Sandra sat quietly for a moment, deep in thought. Then she offered the two joiners an additional bonus of five pounds each if they would arm themselves with their claw-hammers and mallets and hound the creator of mechanical horses and confusion right out of her life, up the drive, and away into his own depraved universe. Being men of little culture, short on sympathy for those who did not, in their estimation, do an honest day's work, they immediately agreed and rose from their knees in the crater, weapons dangling from their strong, corded hands.

McHugh left, his last support gone.

"So it is a clarinet, never mind. We can make do. Anyone play the viola? No? It doesn't matter. We can compensate with guitar. One thing though, no Chinese Blocks. I haven't scored any goddamned Chinese Blocks. Shall we give it a whirl? Is it tea-time yet? Can you get those Devon Cream Teas up here or are we too far north? You see, the knife flashing down is represented by this trill which I would have preferred on the flute, but the clarinet will do. Mr Pilsudski, would you play the kazoo for a while until I can sort the orchestration out?"

Mr Pilsudski tried to tell the ex-composer that it was, as yet, impossible to proceed with this scene as they had no words to go with it.

"Keerist, you're being held up for words? I can give you words."

"I think Ben might be a bit sensitive if you started writing scenes for his play . . ."

"Look man, I'm a writer, that's what I *am* now. I used to be a composer. So there's no problem. Who is better fitted to write a libretto to this scene than the man who wrote the goddamned music? Doesn't that make sense? Give me ten bucks and two hours in a quiet bar and you'll have your words."

Pilsudski shook his head doubtfully.

"I couldn't do that to Ben."

"Jeeeezus, he runs off in a fit of pique and you just sit around waiting for him to come back. How long have we got? Not long. Today is half over. Can you get hamburgers here, I mean genuine hamburgers? Joan honey, could you take me up to a place in town where we could get a decent hamburger?"

Joan Earth hugged the arm of the ex-composer. In the

71

sacrifice scene she had been given the part of lead contralto, the high priestess. Originally it had been scored for a bass-baritone but as soon as Jules Stack had seen the superb carnal shape of the actress and vaguely remembered his flying contact with its pneumatic splendour at the Normality party, he had started hearing different sounds coming from the throat of this character.

"When you say that the second major musical scene you've arranged is a dramatization of a ship-launch, who did you have in mind for Empress of Syria? Isn't she the one who actually cracks the amphora on the prow of the quinquereme and sings the long aria about expanding world trade?" Joan purred silkily.

"Right on," the ex-composer cackled, squeezing her hand. "And now that I'm re-writing the whole goddamned play you can do the part of St Paul's Amazonian lieutenant in 'The Crush the Christians' Crusade'."

"Will I have to strap up my right tit to fire arrows?" Joan Earth asked, ready for anything. "I don't mind. I'll do it if you want me to."

"Hell no, Joan, what do you think I am? Some kind of spoilsport?"

"Can I wear long black lace-up boots?"

"Wear a goddamned stormtrooper's helmet if you want to baby."

"Come on, Jules, be serious."

"I am serious. Theatre has to be liberated honey. Set free! Brought up to date. One thing we don't need is junk on stage. Which brings me to this shit idea about a mechanical horse. That's out. That's just a goddamned gimmick!"

"How am I going to get rid of him?" Pilsudski demanded.

Weldon Stack scratched his nose, eyeing the desperate director with less than favour.

"Peter, give him a chance. He's only been here for a day."

"No, Weldon, you give me a chance. Or ask *him* to give me a chance. I didn't realize that he was a megalomaniac as well as his other hang-ups and problems. He's busy inserting every piece of music he's ever written into Ben's play and chopping out all the text he can. Weldon, it's a take-over bid. You didn't tell me that your brother was such a dynamic character. Also you didn't tell me that he was unconscious of other people's feelings. If Ben comes back and finds out what your brother is trying to do, he'll probably kill him."

"Let me talk to Jules . . ." the front-of-house manager began.

"No, Weldon. You must send him somewhere else."

"But Jules is paranoid! This could push him over the edge. He'd never get over it."

"What about me? Weldon, I'm very worried. Your brother has had a great impact on all of us. He has alienated my writer, who is also my friend, and he is now busy alienating my whole cast. Tonight he is taking the Equity deputy out to dinner at the flat of one of Ben's girlfriends, or should I say ex-girlfriends. I don't know how North America contained your brother for so long. Now I know why the Indians live on reservations miles from anywhere. They're hiding from him."

Weldon Stack shook his bush of hair.

"I must admit that he's got worse. We packed him off to Canada because he was trying to take over the Royal College of Music, Glyndebourne and the London Symphony Orchestra, using the same tactics. But then he was quite cunning about it, even skilful . . . Now? Well, he goes in for the direct approach and that never works in the arts, does it?"

Pilsudski shrugged. The front-of-house manager could see from the set of the broad jaw and the set expression in the green eyes of the Australian that there was no point in arguing. Jules Stack would have to go. The return of the prodigal prodigy had not worked.

"Will you use his music?" Weldon Stack asked humbly. "For my sake. It will help me keep him on an even keel."

"Weldon, your brother would not know an even keel if he fell over one. If I can find places to use it, I might. But I can't promise anything. I'm more concerned about Ben at the moment. I don't know where he is, but I can guess how he's feeling. We have a responsibility towards writers you know, Weldon. Without them we directors cannot exist. They have to be cared for, even protected sometimes. I believe in Ben, you see."

Weldon Stack fingered the enormous knot in his day-glo pink tie.

"Ben will be all right," he murmured nervously. "He's

having a rough time with Beryl I know, but things will work out."

Pilsudski picked up his script, deliberately sliding a thick wedge of tattered beer-stained musical notation out on to Weldon Stack's bunk.

"Weldon, the time is coming when we're all going to have to stand up and be counted. Whatever happens, I'm behind Ben, and this new play. I know that Sean and Glenda are doing their best to screw the whole scene up for us. All this will come out in the open soon enough. Just see you jump the right way, towards the theatre, not away from it. With you by my side I'd take on the Warsaw Pact and the White House in a diplomatic sort-out and come out smiling. But if you go in the other direction, I'll have your balls for a bonnet-ornament."

Weldon Stack went sombre. The lids of his strange slavonic eyes crinkled into hooded creases and corners and his upper lip slid out, pensive.

"I'm not as sure about Ben as you are, Peter. Somehow he's not . . . properly equipped. He worries me. I keep thinking he's going to explode. Do you know what I mean?"

"No."

"You know that if *The Blinding Light* bombs, you're finished? Sean will have a free hand with the board. The council were here yesterday, trying to get *The Unfathomable Grass* taken off . . ."

"Let the council go and screw themselves," Pilsudski snapped. "We'll never create anything through councils and county arsecreepers. We have a responsibility to make this broken-down heap of scrap-iron work as a theatre, as an innovator, a breaker of new ground, a place where new things are born, new experiences, new images and ideas. It's not going to be a can for their clapped-out morals while I'm director. When they walk in through those doors Weldon, I'm going to see to it that they run up against truths no one has ever had the guts to tell the featherbedded and shiftless Pom bastards before! I'm going to bang the bastards back in the womb and make them be born all over again. And I'll win. In the end, I'll win."

Weldon Stack raised his eyebrows, coolly quizzical, refusing to be swayed.

Inside his head a prophetic calculator was at work, estimating the results of many permutations of could-be, might-be, will-be and should-be. In the sum total Pilsudski stood amongst the ruins of several fractions and numbers—but the front-of-house manager could not see who was standing with him, and where the triumph was to be.


## thirteen · A Cry for Help

McHugh had often thought about suicide. It offered not only an escape from Beryl, but also an *explanation*. From the moment he had met the determined, mercenary redhead, he had been doomed. Marrying her had been the first step in self-slaughter. The vicar had cocked the firing-mechanism, the guests at the wedding feast had aimed the deadly barrel at the bridegroom's heart, and now, several years later, *The Blinding Light* was going to pull the trigger and send McHugh into an early but friendly grave. For such an error of love it was right that a man should die. What other redemption was there? He had loved Beryl, but not lived up to her expectations. He had not changed in the direction of the upward swing of the graph but had jumped off the graph altogether. Beryl could not forgive him. He could not forgive himself. If he had been right to pursue this writer's life, why was it that everyone had deserted him? Surely McHugh had been wrong. He had hunted the mighty elephant in the jungle of the arts, and found only a caterpillar. For that was McHugh—suspended, all his beauty still folded inside a dis-figured and evil-appearing body. Beryl had repeatedly called him evil. When he had let his hair grow she had said that it made him look evil. When he had started wearing a Star of David round his neck she had mocked it as an evil charm. When, in his despair, he had groaned in his sleep in their double-bed with the white imitation leather headboard, she had said that it was because he was having evil dreams. For hours McHugh had stared into his shaving mirror, searching for the tell-tale signs. Were his incisor teeth getting any longer? Was his nose curving down to meet his chin? Were his eyes growing craftier? Eventually he gave up shaving and grew a beard. Beryl had immediately condemned the beard as evil. Now, as McHugh parked the roaring Midget on the road below Cwm Fell and unloaded his haversack of suicide equipment, he knew in his heart that Beryl had been right. He was evil and must be destroyed. What he was doing to the minds of those innocent people who saw his plays or read his poems and stories was tantamount to mental murder. They could only suffer from any contact with his ideas or images. He was glad that everyone had deserted him. It had brought the truth home. At least he had the courage to carry out the self-murder. Of that he had no doubt. McHugh could depend on the strength of his mind, if not its moral quality.

With the haversack on his back he crossed the bridge over the beck and marched along the track through the valley. It was a fine afternoon. Sheep grazed on the pastures, birds sang softly in the trees, the sky carried high banks of pure white cloud, a breeze cooled his cheek. It was a good day to die.

In the glove compartment of the Midget he had left three letters—one to Beryl, one to his mother, and one to Pilsudski. All of them were brief and to the point. Not an atom of sentiment or self-pity warped their clear, direct sentences. He could not go on because the world did not want him to go on. He had been democratically voted out of life. So be it. McHugh did not want to be a burden on society. He had tried and failed.

A farmer passed by with his sheep-dog. The animal leapt up at McHugh, nuzzling his hand. The farmer curtly called it to his side and tramped on, regardless of the sad hiker. McHugh pondered: if he had said good morning to me, offered a friendly word, would I have changed my mind?

He decided that it would take more than a shepherd to bring this lamb back to the fold. On, up the first gradients of the track by the waterfalls where the beck bubbled over boulders, past rowan trees. His heart started to beat stronger and he lengthened his stride. Over his head wheeled upland crows with the occasional seagull gliding in from the coast. A small brown rabbit broke from the cover of fresh green fern and shot along the path. Far above him he heard the drone of an aeroplane. The path turned to the left, under a buttress of exposed rock. In the distance McHugh saw the first glint of the tarn, his destination and his destiny.

His mother had tried to make him believe in destiny. Until now McHugh had rejected the idea as slavish and illogical. Within himself was the power of choice. He was the taker of roads, of chances, of opportunities: no other agency forced a free soul to travel these ways. Now McHugh veered towards his mother's interpretation of life. He could understand the old lady's resignation, her stoical acceptance of pain and trouble. Either one was blessed with good luck, or one shared the lot of the majority—the shitty end of the stick. Here was where McHugh had gone wrong. He had believed himself to be *different*. He wasn't, the fool! He shook his head, humping the haversack higher on to his shoulders.

The strides were steady now and his breath was rhythmical as he climbed the last fifty feet up the twisting path to drop down again and see the tarn spread out at his feet. It lay in the mountain basin, a long, still pool of slow reflections and silver, quiet. Even the birds sounded far away. McHugh paused on the head of an outcrop. Here was oblivion and a secret death. They would never find him here. Running his eye along the opposite shore he saw the spot which he had selected from his memory of the tarn's topography. It was a low cliff which hung over a deep part of the tarn. He had swum there, diving down to find the bottom and failing. With clear light and water, there was no bottom to be found. McHugh would lie there, in peace.

Turning to the north he walked around the edge of the tarn towards the place.

When he arrived, McHugh sat down on the edge of the cliff and smoked a cigarette, staring into the black depths. He was not afraid. Fear had left him. Tremors of *doubt* shook him though, doubt as to whether he was right to cop out at this stage, surrender, allow Jules Stack to walk all over him. This was not in character. It burned him that the ex-composer might think that McHugh had run away from any confrontation. Too late. Jules Stack had been the last straw, that's all. What was a last straw? Perhaps Jules Stack might write him a lament called "The Last Straw" and play it at the opening night? Then McHugh recalled that Jules Stack had stopped composing. He shuddered to think what old piece might be adapted for the occasion.

From the haversack he took his leotard. He had bought this one-piece garment to do movement class with the actors. Pilsudski had been going through an ensemble phase when he wanted everyone in the Dramacart to do things together.

For three weeks Weldon Stack, McHugh, Fred and Bert and Lulu had been forced to join in the morning session of eurhythmics and voice-training, clad in leotards. Only when Bert, sullen and uncooperative from the start, had declared that as he was no fookin intellectual he was not going to dress or behave like one, had the enlightened and unifying scheme collapsed. There was an irony in the fact that Mc-Hugh was going to use this uniform of the theatre as part of his suicide. As he struggled into it and started thrusting stones inside, shaking them down into his legs, he was forced to smile grimly. Beryl had said that he looked evil in his leotard. Slowly he filled the garment until it bulged in every limb. On the cliff, outlined against the clear water, McHugh began to take on the appearance of a human cairn.

Using a length of thick rope he tied his ankles together.

With difficulty he fastened his big leather belt with the brass buckle round his waist. From it hung two twenty-five pound weights borrowed from the flat-supports of the set of *The Unfathomable Grass*. Finally he took out a small sack attached to a chain and dog-collar. Fastening the collar round his neck he bent over and filled the sack with rocks, then straightened up, holding the sack to his chest.

With great care he inched himself to the edge of the cliff.

One last look around the heavens.

A last ear to the birds.

A last sweet breath of the earth's air.

"Excuse me sir," called the police sergeant as he rose from the bed of ferns where he had been drowsing, his mind full of the brilliant dialogue and action which he had seen on the stage of the Dramacart Moving Theatre the previous evening. "Aren't you Mr B. McHugh, the well-known writer?"

McHugh stiffened, the rocks chinking inside the leotard. He could not turn his head to face the direction from which the voice was coming. Rocks shifted from the back of the leotard towards the front. He felt his centre of gravity moving forward. He tilted.

"I suppose you're trying out a few ideas for your next play. Quiet spot this. A great favourite with artists you know. What is it to be, science-fiction?"

McHugh tried to call out but the dog collar was choking him.

What was that he had heard the voice say?

The *well-known* writer!

"Well, sir, I'd like to thank you for a wonderful evening. I went to see your play *The Unfathomable Grass* and I've never enjoyed myself so much. I don't care what other people say, sir, as far as I'm concerned you're a flaming genius. That female p.c. is absolutely real. What's the point of writing plays which don't get *through* to people's subconscious mind? Where do they think the criminal tendency starts? It's right there, isn't it? In the subconscious mind. All right, so what you've shown us there *seems* unusual, maybe a bit far-fetched. But only to them, sir, not to me. I have to face these situations. And to say that it's obscene is ridiculous. I've looked up the legal definition of obscene in my textbooks, sir, and I can tell you, it's laughable. They don't know what it means! What's obscene to one person isn't obscene to another, not necessarily. I mean, there's nothing in your play that titivates, is there sir? Even with that fine big girl playing the female p.c., she's very good incidentally, sir, a first-rate performer. No, sir, what I found in your play was an alternative way of looking at things. I've been lying up here—it's my day off—looking at the sky, enjoying the peace and quiet, and wondering whether I'm in the right business. But if I jack it all in, you'll get some bloke who has this old-fashioned idea of obscenity at the station and time will stand still in Orrestwater for another hundred years. So I'm in a bit of a quandary, sir. What do you think I should do? Stay in the force and try to improve things, get them up to date, or get out altogether and find a new job? You don't give lessons in writing do you? I've done a bit, you know, stories about petty criminals, sheep-rustlers and people who maltreat their pets, but I never get it really right. What I find is that my characters can't talk. I think the dialogue is the thing, don't you, sir? If you can master the dialogue then you're half-way there, aren't you? I'll tell you what, there was one exchange in your play that I loved. I can remember it word for word. Did I laugh? I laughed fit to bust. You know that bit where Basil says 'Have you ever tried to set fire to a paddy-field?' I nearly died. How do you think up these things? Do they just come naturally or do you have to work on them for hours, experimenting, trying different ways of saying it?"

McHugh tipped forward as the leotard altered shape, all

79

the stones from the chest and armpits slumping down into the lower abdomen. Suddenly he did not want to die. That voice was calling him back. A friend. A believer. McHugh's head craned over the depths, the sack swinging out. Desperately he clawed at the collar. He managed to get the spike out of the hole in the collar. Too late. He was going! The clouds reeled over his head. Letting out a strangled cry of hopeless terror, McHugh snatched the collar away. The leotard burst open at the front spilling the stones into the lake. McHugh stepped back from death, the twenty-five pound weights banging on his hips.

"See what I mean? It's technique, isn't it sir? Timing. I couldn't have done that in a month of Sundays. Would you like to share my packed lunch? I've got a few of Mrs Blakeney's flaky-pastry sausage-rolls and a flask of tea. Shall we sit down sir? Take the weight off your feet?"

The police sergeant held out a hand and helped McHugh to sit down. While the writer recovered from his near pass with Death, the grizzled and companionable lawman undid the rope around his ankles and dragged the ragged remnants of the leotard off, casting the old skin far away into the cheated tarn.

God Perkins and Fred cantered down to the boundary fence of the car-park and back again. The engineer had welded two extra sets of baffles into the silencing system and developed an exhaust-filter through the tail, using countless layers of wire wool and spun glass. God Perkins was almost equine, quiet, sweet-smelling, and obedient. To keep the secret of the new theatrical machine, Pilsudski had insisted that Fred only exercise God Perkins under cover of an all-enveloping canvas groundsheet. As the mechanical horse pranced over the car-park, the groundsheet billowed and flapped like the blazoned coat of a knight's charger. Interested spectators leant over the fence and discussed the strange apparition of an oily man riding a large piece of animated canvas.

"See!" Pilsudski pointed at the slack jaws and puzzled expressions of the watchers. "They're unsettled. It's something they haven't seen before. They're frightened, shocked. When they're in that state, that's the time to strike! Ben's play will cut right through all the old camp trash, sweep it off the stage! We'll start a revolution! See that?"

Two old ladies turned and scurried away as God Perkins galloped dangerously near, the canvas flapping, Fred hanging over the hidden neck trying out the Red Indian trick of shooting from under the horse's head. As Fred peered round the great steel skull under its hood of groundsheet, he lost his grip and fell to the earth, his war-whoop cut short. God Perkins galloped on and ran into a tree, limbs threshing. Spectators clambered over the fence to help the fallen man and beast but Fred was already on his feet, shooing them away as he groped for the controls under the canvas.

"I'm all right. You mustn't come too near. This is top secret. A new weapon for the Navy. We could have done with it in Gibraltar in 1943, I can tell you. Go on, go home now. There's nothing to see. I'm all right."

Unwillingly, the spectators climbed back over the fence and watched the controller of the magic groundsheet lead it back to the theatre. Most of them had heard rumours about the Dramacart from the keepers of their boarding-houses and hotel managers. Hints had been dropped that the odd collection of furniture lorries and caravans contained more than a troupe of travelling actors and their performances—perverse rituals, black magic, orgies perhaps—but no one, to date, had imagined that it hid a new secret weapon for the Navy. That evening Fred's ride was the subject of many discussions as the tourists talked through courses of Lancashire hot-pot and sprouts, deep apple-pie and custard followed by triangles of prawn cheese and coffee, in the guest-houses and hotels around Orrestwater.

That night *The Unfathomable Grass* played to a full house. In the interval, after the majority of the audience had walked out, the remainder were to be seen creeping round to the back of the theatre, looking under groundsheets, behind caravans, under the jacked-up floor of the auditorium. Bert found a man and his wife hiding in the properties store. They were examining a large flat which had a rocket painted on it. It had been part of a set for a pantomime of an up-dated *Sinbad the Sailor*. While trying to eject them, Bert was treated to a severe grilling by the husband who claimed to be a retired draughtsman from Vickers at Barrow-in-Furness, manufacturers of the British nuclear submarine.

When Bert reported this incident to Sean and Glenda he was surprised to find that neither of them appeared to be concerned. In fact Sean smiled knowingly, while Glenda merely lightened her rigid frown of disappointment (for she was still struck mute from her downgrading).

"Sean, I'm wondering whether I should stay on here," Bert confessed. "It's not like the old days. No one wants to do the job they're paid for. Where's the old spirit? I can remember the nights when we sat around the camp-fire with spuds in the ashes, roasting sausages, drinking beer and telling stories about Sir Henry Irving. None of that goes on since these fookin intellectuals came here. And you bringing in more of the buggers every day! It doesn't make sense. I used to like the charades we played and the old folk-songs. All right, I haven't got a great voice, but it's not bad for the kind of songs I sing . . ."

"You've got a fine voice, Bert," Sean consoled the stage-manager. "I've often mentioned it to Pilsudski."

"It's not an intellectual voice, but it's all right."

"Of course it is."

Bert blinked at the general manager, his fingers busy rolling a cigarette.

"I don't know what to do, Sean. This place is all upside down to me. I'd rather I was with the old jolly vagabonds, all mucking in and enjoying ourselves. Do you remember the night Bill Gort let down the tyres on the chemical-toilet caravan? That was a lark eh? No fun like that since the fookin intellectuals got here. I blame you Sean. You brought this Pilsudski here. Now I've got the fookin public interrogating me in my own properties van. They don't trust us any more. Where's all the parties we used to have at the Mother's Union? There were a few fit pieces of grumble at them dos . . ."

Gently Sean eased Bert out of his purple caravan and closed the door. The general manager was exhausted. All day he had tried to get Glenda to speak. She would not. Now they faced a night together in the double bunk of the purple caravan. Sean needed her. Would it be another night where the prince and the princess were separated by the sword lying from pillow to footboard?

Outside he heard McHugh's car, the exhaust bellowing.

Sean's temper snapped.

Even for his *own play* this man would make no allowances! In the auditorium there were people who had paid good money to see the workings of McHugh's crazed mind, and the writer could not respect that contract!

The general manager flung open the door of his purple caravan and roared out a stream of foul oaths, words that sprang to his tongue from a long-hidden cistern in his soul. Glenda blanched and turned away, shocked.

"Now then! Now then!" the police sergeant said reprovingly as he stepped out of the Midget, wagging a finger under Sean's nose. "We want none of that obscenity here!"

## fourteen · Reconciliation and Rehabilitation

Dearden Ryan and Geoffrey Block sat at the polished copper-topped Britannia table in the saloon bar of the Rainbow in Curdog. Surrounded by hunting prints and horns, they ate cottage-pie and peas, sipped pints of fizzy bitter, and discussed the antecedents of Ben McHugh.

"Your suspicions were quite correct," Sean nodded heavily. "He did play Rugby Union."

"How did you find that out?" Dearden Ryan inquired with interest.

Geoffrey Block tutted with exasperation and removed his lace cuffs from the cottage-pie. Even though this pub had all the plush county trimmings of a jocular print showing fat squires smoking long clay pipes, yet it was not London. Somehow it malfunctioned. There was an odour about it. Lavender polish.

It was provincial.

"McHugh really showed his team colours," Sean munched enthusiastically, "he behaved very badly. I mean, we all know writers and directors have rows about interpretation, it goes on all the time, but I think McHugh is the first writer I've ever heard of who's brought the police in on his side."

Dearden Ryan lit a king-size menthol cigarette with a gold ring round the filter. He did not want to over-react. The mood that London must always communicate to the shires was a knowing, intelligent cool. Also he felt uneasy under the critical eye of several heavily set men in tweeds and deer-stalkers who were running down the homosexual leanings of contemporary society while drinking gin and orange at the other end of the bar. Adjusting his address, suppressing the tell-tale high notes of alarm, he asked Sean to expand on the story.

"Pilsudski called in a composer to do the music. He's quite a go-ahead sort, wants to get working, get involved. Anyway, McHugh had wandered off in one of his ridiculous piques and the composer—he's a Canadian and very *avant-garde*, you know, industrial sounds, barges under iron bridges, jet-aircraft, compressed-air drills, warping sheet-metal, that kind of thing—he took the opportunity to do a few experiments, try out a couple of ideas. Nothing irrevocable. No damage done. And Pilsudski let him. He stood by and let him. Later on he said it was to see what this composer was really after, test him, but I know better. Pilsudski was getting ready to ditch McHugh. There's a split there all right. Pilsudski's fed up with McHugh's private life interfering with his *art*."

"Are you telling me that McHugh's private life is not *conventional*?" Geoffrey Block asked worriedly. "It would be far better if it was. One of the standard features of a *nouveau riche* on the up-and-up is a manifest desire to be accepted. They conform like mad."

Glenda laughed, a merry trill which escaped from her full pink throat like the song of a shrike.

"Good lord, Geoffrey, he's absolutely *straight*. No, you mustn't think that he's adventurous or interested in exploring new territory as far as sexual relationships are concerned. It's just that his marriage is breaking up."

"Ah, that's better," Geoffrey Block sighed with relief. "That is conventional."

"His wife is a schoolteacher," Sean chipped in, a wry grin on his bearded countenance. "That standard enough for you?"

"Better and better," Dearden chuckled, rubbing his hands. "Carry on with the contretemps."

Glenda took up the tale, her small brown eyes shining.

"There was a performance of our current box-office disaster, McHugh's *The Unfathomable Grass*, on at the time, and the composer had taken the cast down to the shore of the lake with Pilsudski. In the experiments that the Canadian was conducting he had a sequence which was to accompany the actual moment when St Paul falls off his horse on the road to Damascus. We haven't got the live horse in yet as it would be too expensive, and the mechanical horse is under repair at the moment . . ."

Geoffrey Block and Dearden Ryan stared at each other over their plates of cottage-pie, wide-eyed.

"So old Murphy Winspear was carrying Joe Woodhead on his back along the shore, and the rest of the company were practising a musical sequence, having dived out in the interval . . ."

"You mean they rehearse *in the interval?*" Geoffrey Block spluttered through a mouthful of gassy bitter. "What does the Equity deputy say about that?"

"Geoffrey, he knows the fix we're in. Give him credit for some common sense. We're doing our best to put on a reasonable show of this bloody awful play. He doesn't obstruct theatrical experiment. Well, the composer had two sieves of gravel, a tape-recording of whales speaking to each other underwater, Japanese wind-bells which we had lent them, an African thumb-piano, the hub-caps off the Bedford, five jew's harps . . . and I tell you, it was very interesting, wasn't it Glenda? Quite a fascinating sound they were making. The composer was conducting them through some very intricate rhythms. Just before the interval had started, up rolls McHugh—no silencer on his car as usual—with this police sergeant who'd been laying his wife . . ."

"Whose wife?" Geoffrey Block asked faintly.

"McHugh's wife."

"The schoolteacher?"

"Yes."

"Christ, there's an Establishment liaison if you like!" Dearden Ryan shook his head grimly. "What a set-up."

"Were they fighting?" Geoffrey Block frowned, remembering the useful anonymity of the metropolis where the professions could mix unnoticed and unregistered. "I presume they were hostile to each other?"

"Not at all. They were very chummy. Both of them were horribly drunk, arms round each other. McHugh had been drinking with the policeman all afternoon in some pub. They abused me, they abused Glenda, they abused a lot of people who were walking away from the play—our regular quota of discerning patrons—then they went to find Pilsudski. They found the composer rehearsing the company in a beautiful piece of chorus work, I think it's called 'The

Ontario Power Line Pulsations' in which they have to make this *bzzz bzzz bzzz* sound like rain on high-voltage cables, you've heard the sound. Pilsudski was with them but he was sitting to one side, letting Jules conduct the buzzing while he worked out the moves that would create a pylon effect, I think it involved standing on shoulders and that kind of thing . . . the next thing we know is that McHugh crash-tackles the composer—rugby union *sans doute*, and the policeman arrests him."

Dearden Ryan frowned, examining Sean's eyes for tell-tale signs of undue strain or mental breakdown. The general manager had obviously cracked up. These were the imaginings of an overheated and plagued brain.

"Yes, Sean," he said gently, patting the general manager's hand so the men in deerstalkers flared their nostrils, "we'll sort it all out for you."

"And Pilsudski just sat there, cheering them on!" Sean added. "They attack a creative artist under his nose and he encourages them. The man's a killer!"

"Sean we'll have to go into this whole business very thoroughly and prepare a case, quite free from prejudice . . . (here he glanced at Glenda's Fair Isle poncho for the bump. It had gone.) . . . Firstly, there's the script for *The Blinding Light*, we must have a look at that. We should see this play of McHugh's that people keep walking out of, maybe meet his wife, talk to someone on the local council. But as far as the company is concerned, we're just here for a visit. All right? Just checking on artistic standards, the usual thing."

Sean nodded his agreement. He had caught the note of disapproval in Dearden Ryan's voice, noted the sharpness of his eyes and the wrinkles at the base of his nose. Always conscious of the risk inherent in asking the Theatrefund to pry into the life of a theatre far from the hub of the wheel, Sean had calculated an initial reaction of this nature. As the general manager he should never have allowed the situation to develop this far: it had got beyond his control. With all the forces of social reaction massed to capture the theatre for propaganda purposes—especially the articulate *nouveau riche*—Sean had dropped his guard, been too innocent and trusting. Now the Dramacart was a bear-pit of passions, full of people going in different directions. There was no policy but confusion, no aim but chaos. Yesterday, as he had watched the composer being knocked from his podium and brought crashing to the ground, the general manager had shuddered. The tall were always weak in the middle. It was the small, earth-bound minds that survived, the rats and moles, the diggers and gnawers. Both Pilsudski and McHugh were of the rodent breed—without principle, hungry, and armed with a nose for the blood that streams from collapsed ambition. They had the advantage of being anarchists; men with no conscience, violent men, predators on the hapless and benumbed.

Jules Stack smiled wryly at Harriet from behind the bars of the Orrestwater police station's single cell.

"You know these bastards even took my stick away from me? And my passport. McHugh's goddamned friend has hidden it somewhere and is getting me charged as an illegal immigrant. For Chrissake, I went to Winchester! How can a guy who went to Winchester be an illegal immigrant? Didn't you bring me a basket of food? I thought everyone brought prisoners a basket of food. There's some traditions that are worth keeping up."

Harriet touched the ex-composer's lined, battered face through the bars, a deep, womanly compassion at work in her heart. With patience, tact, and a lot of love, this man could be saved from himself. There was a vacancy coming up for a Helper Grade Three at the laboratories. Jules was more than capable of doing the job. If the police kept him locked up for a week or so he might dry out, feel lonely, look to Harriet for rehabilitation . . .

"Do you think you could get me a few beers or a bottle of something? Couldn't you bake a cake and put a bottle in it? Christ, this place is boring. I thought they had television in British gaols now. I don't see any television here. That bastard police sergeant won't even lend me any of his books. That guy has got more books on obscenity and censorship than any lawyer. Do all the fuzz over here get so *involved*?"

"I'll come and see you tomorrow," Harriet said softly.

"Don't forget the cake."

"I'd rather not, Jules. It's against the Law. I respect the Law."

"Christ, you see how the Law respects me? This is a

frame-up! That bastard McHugh has set me up, him and his kinky friend at the desk. You know that sergeant keeps bringing me poems and stories he's written and asking for my opinion? He's in the wrong job."

"He's not the only one," Harriet smiled warmly. "I know someone else who should find himself."

"Anyway, I've given him some of my stuff to read as well. I tell you something. I can write a damn sight better than him. He's all over the place. No plot. That's his trouble. No plot. No dynamic. If he kept off dialogue and tried to sort out the action, then he might get somewhere."

Harriet left. She passed Weldon Stack on his way in.

"How is he?" Weldon asked.

"Wonderful," Harriet whispered. "I think it will do him a world of good."

"He's not depressed?"

"No, he's just coming to terms with himself. Does he want children?"

Weldon Stack brushed at his giant bush of hair and paused. The idea of his brother as a father was deeply disturbing. Yet this girl, obviously sane and well balanced, was actively contemplating a permanent union with Jules. Weldon Stack put a hand inside his jacket-pocket.

"Some advice. Will you give me some advice? See this?" He showed Harriet an envelope. "This is a writ of habeas corpus. I can get Jules out of here. The solicitor also told me that the arresting officer appears before a tribunal next Friday and is being suspended from duty pending investigation. He is not the man he used to be. But do we want Jules out? Might not it be to our mutual advantage to keep him here for a while longer?"

"As far as I'm concerned, yes," Harriet answered. "It will give me time to make arrangements for his interview. He must be sober for the interview. Do you really think he's ready to settle down?"

Weldon Stack nodded fervently.

"The best thing that could happen to him."

"Then let's leave him here to sweat it out," Harriet said. "At least we'll know where he is."

The following morning, Pilsudski called a company meeting. When Sean, Glenda, Geoffrey Block and Dearden Ryan arrived they were told to wait outside while certain questions of artistic policy were discussed.

"You see what I mean?" Sean said grimly. "Locked out of my own theatre."

The drama officers raised their eyebrows and walked away.

"Your authority has certainly been whittled away, Sean," Dearden Ryan murmured sympathetically. "Not so sure that you should have let that happen. Why didn't you insist? Just walk in?"

"I'm not a confrontation specialist. As far as I'm concerned, the play's the thing. All I ask for is justice."

Glenda pressed her rich lips together, dreaming of the evening performance. When the drama officers actually witnessed the walk-outs, heard the shouting of the enraged customers demanding their money back at the Moorish window, they would swing towards the side of the management. Faced with an abortive piece of raffish lunacy like *The Unfathomable Grass*, they would have to commit themselves to the right cause.

In the auditorium, McHugh had just sat down after a long speech of apology. He had apologized to Murphy Winspear and Joe Woodhead. He had apologized to Joan Earth. He had apologized to Pilsudski. He had apologized to everyone. The crucial moment of his apology came when he had to apologize for having a part in the arbitrary incarceration of the ex-composer, Jules Stack. This flagrant alliance with the Establishment had enraged the actors and made them doubt McHugh's integrity. However, when McHugh had explained to them that the sergeant was in the throes of a metamorphosis from authority-figure to bohemian artist, and the story of the attempted suicide had been told, backed up by Weldon Stack's assurance that the legal intricacies had been sorted out and his brother was now with an aunt in Edinburgh for a few days, McHugh was forgiven. In return he produced a part as St Paul's long-lost sister for Joan Earth, a magnificent speech for the Christian about to be castrated with giant pincers for the Equity deputy, plus a supply of stronger subtexts for the smaller parts. Only Fred was disappointed. Equity had instructed the theatre not to allow him to either speak or move, except as an integral fixture of God Perkins. Only in case of extreme emergency would he be allowed to dismount or adopt a separate posture to that of sitting in the talking saddle. Fred had to be a mute prop.

"Right, now we can get down to business!" Pilsudski grinned, waving his arms in the air and shaking his lank hair. "A week to work it through, and this shitty deal on the millionaire's island on Saturday. This is a fantastic challenge. Let's get on with it, eh? We're in it to win it!"

Fired with a fresh enthusiasm, the company left the meeting, leaving McHugh and Pilsudski alone.

"Well, Ben, who's your friend?" Pilsudski called over the empty seats. "Who backed you from the beginning? Who had faith in you?"

McHugh sat up, his script clutched in his hand. He knew that Pilsudski was about to try and stir him up emotionally, toss across a flight of grappling-hooks and take the writer's soul in tow. McHugh assumed a fierce control of his facial muscles and hrrmphed deep in his throat.

"This is going to be a great play, Ben. We'll look back on today as a turning-point. They wanted you out, Ben, but I talked them round."

"Thanks, Peter," McHugh muttered, "thanks a lot."

"I'll make it good Ben. We'll have those metropolitan bastards streaming up the M6 in convoy for a chance to buy an option. *The Blinding Light* is going to be the play of the year. I'll get all the London critics up. We'll accept no excuses this time. They can shift their fat arses to go and see some camp trash in the back-room of a knocking-shop in Chalk Farm so they can come here or I'll crucify the bastards in the *Stage*. This is the gathering of a new wave Ben, a tidal wave!"

Pilsudski got off the stage and walked up the aisle to where McHugh was sitting, a pillar of self-control, an idol of rigid patience. The artistic director put an arm round the writer's neck and squeezed.

"It all comes from you, Ben. This is your heart's blood. Where would we be without you? From now on, the play's the thing. The phase of throwing ideas back and forth is over. I tried out a few thoughts, knocked them around a bit —Weldon's brother was one of them but that didn't work— and now we're down to basic issues. The word. The holy word. Wait and see what I'll come up with Ben. I won't let you down."

90

McHugh met the bold eyes of the Australian. He groaned inwardly.

God Almighty, what could you do with this man?

He drove you mad, tortured you, betrayed you, and then proved that you could not live without him. Resistance was pointless. Pilsudski would win in the end because of his pure energy.


## fifteen · Doubts and Fears

Geoffrey Block and Dearden Ryan watched the afternoon rehearsal of *The Blinding Light* through two holes which Sean had bored through the back of the foyer in order to keep a managerial eye on exactly what was being done in *his* theatre. Occasionally they consulted their copy of the script, lent by a disgruntled Bert who had commented that he could not make head nor tail of the fookin intellectual nonsense. When the rehearsal stopped for a tea-break, Sean invited the drama officers back to his purple caravan for a cup of Darjeeling. The men from the Theatrefund were thoughtful, withdrawn and distant as they sat on the colourful blankets under sprays of dried grasses and heads of spangled hogweed. Sean was patient. He allowed them to drink their tea in peace. At his side, Glenda was restless. She was desperate to know what they thought of McHugh's play.

Finally Geoffrey Block put her out of her misery.

"What is worrying about the play is the choice of subject. St Paul is not entirely approved of at the moment, even by the Anglican Church. Very suspect. I heard him referred to as a moral Nazi and a male chauvinist by a curate at a St Martin-in-the-Fields lunch-time concert the other week. He's far too hard-line on sex for contemporary tastes. This God Perkins machine seems to be an instrument of repressive social policies and the sexual *ancien régime*. Don't you agree Dearden?"

Dearden read his tea-leaves with a practised eye.

"McHugh has skilfully disguised his evangelizing for the *nouveau riche* culture and all its appalling aims. You have to hand it to him. Very expert piece of camouflage, only detectable to the trained eye. Here, where I've underlined in red, this is the part which betrays him. See Glenda? No doubt about it."

Dearden pointed to the incriminating dialogue, grimly wise.

"You mean that bit before the pursuit of the Christian minority round and round the revolve?" Glenda said excitedly. "Yes, I know where you mean. I noticed that. Indefensible!"

"Let me see," Geoffrey Block leaned across and studied the script. "Ah, yes, I'd made a mental note to raise that. I think McHugh revealed himself there. Got too close to the surface."

Sean studied the page. He had never admitted to Glenda that there were shades of meaning, symbols, suggestions, sub-texts and psychological twists in all plays that she could see but he could not. His apparatus for detecting social flaws in works of art was inefficient. Much slipped past him, unnoticed. This odd blindness had sometimes created friction between them.

"Can't you see what we mean?" Glenda asked, a note of irritation in her voice. "It's staring you right in the face."

Sean scratched at his beard.

"I think . . . is it this part?" He stabbed with a stubby forefinger.

"No, this section. Honestly, Sean, it sticks out a mile," Glenda snapped.

Sean stared at the lines, following Glenda's finger-nail as she traced it through the damning dialogue between St Paul and God Perkins. Somewhere in the back of his mind a pathetic rebellion arose, tiny mental flags fluttering. He could not see the tell-tale signs, the floating spores of the *nouveau riche* mushroom. With a sigh he crushed the revolt and solemnly nodded.

"I see what you mean. Inescapable."

Dearden Ryan straightened out a piece of hair which had broken out of the lacquer penitentiary of his coiffure.

"Best thing for us to do is send this section down to London. Is there a photocopying machine anywhere in Orrestwater?"

"Yes, at the library. You pop and do that for us now Sean," Glenda instructed the general manager. "I want to show Geoff and Dearden the statistics on the walk-outs in *The Unfathomable Grass*."

Obediently Sean picked up the script and left the purple caravan, got in the Volkswagen, and drove into Orrestwater. When he reached the library he sat in the reference section for a while, pretending to read the *Shooting Times*. On the table in front of him lay the means of destroying McHugh and Pilsudski. Once it got into the hands of the Theatrefund that dialogue, that simple batting back and forth of words, would be akin to playing tennis with a hand-grenade. They would be ruined, obliterated. Sean did not mind that. He hated both men enough to see them shamed before all the theatre industry. What did worry him was that he did not understand what it was in that sequence of dialogue that had given McHugh's game away. This troubled his conscience. He would be bringing down his enemies with a weapon that was secret to the user as well as the used. What had he missed?

"Excuse me," he said to an unshaven, grizzled, genial man who was reading a newspaper at the other side of the table. "Would you do me a favour?"

"If I can," the untidy, humorous fellow replied, a warm smile on his face. "What's up then?"

Sean examined the man. He had seen him before. Probably in town. In the street. *En passant*. He looked helpful, well balanced, a good citizen.

"Would you read this for me and comment upon it?"

"Pass it over then," the friendly man said, holding out an ink-stained hand. "Let's have a gander at it."

"It's the piece underlined in red Biro," Sean explained as he shoved the opened script across. "That's the part I'm interested in."

The police sergeant was enjoying his suspension from duty. He had spent the morning reading through all the back copies of *Plays and Players* and the *Stage*, and was now reading through the social columns in the hope of finding tit-bits about the private lives of writers and whether most of them had confronted Authority at one time or other in their careers, and lost. He had unearthed enough evidence in support of his predicament to make him happy. Now the general manager of the Dramacart Moving Theatre was even asking his opinion about an actual script. Things were going the police sergeant's way that afternoon. Life was definitely improving.

"Not to put too fine a point on it mate, I'd say the man who wrote this was a flaming genius. Listen to the interplay of ideas and emotions, starkly presented, economically realized . . ."

The police sergeant read out the offending piece of theatrical gold.

"I'll do two voices so you can tell the difference. Here, you lot. Never mind reading that trash. Listen to this." The dozy vagrants, pensioners and tramps in the reference section looked up, blearily obeying the command. "The high voice is St Paul. All right? The low voice is God Perkins.

"*(High Voice [St Paul]):* You ask me, how can I hope for better things without God? I answer you that hard work, dedication to my duty, a true respect for the centralized power of a great political empire, and thrift are my God. Already I have *made it*, without God.

*(Low Voice [God Perkins]):* Made it? Made what? What is this magical point in a man's career? You only *make it* when you die and find a life eternal in Heaven. Then O exterminator, you have truly made it.

*(High voice [St Paul]):* I am a success. I am at the top of the tree. In my bank acount in Tarsus, held by the merchant Tyrigia on 42nd Street, I have sufficient funds to last me a lifetime. How did I do this? By doing my job. By being on time. By obeying my superiors and keeping the System working. By devoting my energy and talent to something that works, and has been proved to work. The Roman Empire is my God.

*(Low Voice [God Perkins]):* What a grovelling and unquestioning sycophant you are. Your achievements are nothing. Your strength is as a straw when seen against that of God. The credit of Heaven is what a man needs, not the trashy materialism of Mankind. I will come to you again, the steel of God, the industry of his celestial empire."

The police sergeant gazed over the table at Sean as the audience clapped their horny hands and wheezed enthusiastic cheers.

"Mate, to me that is beautiful. Doesn't it speak up for all of us? Is not this God Perkins the most wonderful idea a

94

man ever had? The Establishment that has a heart? The System which cares? The Big Business which loves us all? It's industry isn't it? God is industry. I don't have to look at the front to know who wrote it. Only one man could write stuff like that. I have had the privilege of talking to him myself, man to man, and helping him out. Mr McHugh, or Ben as he allows me to call him, is the foremost writer of our day."

Sean thanked the police sergeant in an undertone and took the script back. On his way out of the library he paused at the photocopying machine. Behind him he felt Glenda and his own ignorance. They struggled for possession of his soul. Before him were those rough, uncaring, freedom-loving men and the words of McHugh on the air, inspiring the suspended police officer to poetical incantation and the gestures of a Druidical actor.

Sean walked on, the copy untaken, his mind undecided.

"Weldon, we need to know which side you're on."

The front-of-house manager toyed with the brass buckle of his enormous Spanish belt, avoiding Glenda's eyes.

The drama officers eyed the labels on the rack of French wines in the corner of Weldon Stack's caravan, and the empty truffles tins in the waste-paper basket. Disapproval edged into their expressions.

"If I can set the situation out more clearly in your mind Weldon," Dearden Ryan smiled. "One: Pilsudski has effectively alienated his audience. The working class are not coming to the Dramacart . . ."

"Dearden, the working class never go to the theatre. They have never been near the Dramacart or any theatre I have worked in except for the seaside rep in Morecambe, and then we did twenty-five per cent business. Who suggested that the working class wanted to go to the theatre in the first place?"

Geoffrey Block tugged at his lace cuffs in annoyance.

"Weldon, the whole point of subsidized theatre is that it should encourage the working class to leave bingo and the telly and face more demanding realities and genuine experiences in multi-personal relationships." He scowled. "After all, it's their money isn't it? Their taxes. They pay for it."

"Not necessarily. I think you'll find that the middle classes pay for the theatre on their own. Why don't you subsidize bingo? You subsidize the telly one way or the other. The working classes don't *like* theatre. Why should they? I don't like bingo. Why should I?"

Glenda gripped the folds of her burnouse in temper, her knuckles whitening. When Weldon had finished his off-hand, courtly rejection of the drama officer's case, she tore into the front-of-house manager's argument.

"Have you forgotten the block booking we had from the miners' rest-home three weeks ago? The canteen-ladies from Glaxo . . ."

"Fifty seats in all," Weldon interrupted her with a sad, disarming smile. "Glenda, these are fantasies. Most of our customers have got two cars and a bungalow worth more than this theatre."

Sean knocked on the caravan door, then entered. The script was held under his arm. He sized up the situation: Glenda's high colour, Weldon's cool demeanour, the interrogatory combine of the drama officers. Hurriedly he told a lie when Glenda asked if he had mailed off the copy of the guilty section from *The Blinding Light*

"Even with all the evidence we've got, Weldon refuses to commit himself," Glenda fumed at the general manager. "What can we do to persuade him?"

Sean grinned awkwardly, clutching the script tighter to his chest.

"Ed has asked us all over for dinner tonight to discuss the performance of *Dream*. He's especially invited you, Weldon. We told him you were a *bon viveur* and had once had breakfast with Peter O'Toole. He's dying to meet you."

Weldon Stack ran a hand over his great bush of frizzy hair, thinking. He balanced the total effect of his acceptance against the rancour and suspicion that he would generate in Glenda's breast if he refused. Also he could tell Pilsudski about the dinner before, and after, balancing the advantages and disadvantages by passing on intelligence, dropping hints.

"What's the main course?" Weldon demanded with strange uncouthness. "And may my brother come?"

McHugh entered the classroom where Beryl was teaching the third form the conjugation of the verb *pousser*, and held up the summons which he had received from the High Court.

"You can't do this to me," he said loudly. "A woman can't testify against her husband."

The third form hushed, their interested eyes travelling back to Mrs McHugh. Beryl ignored McHugh's presence and wrote 'Nouse poussons' on the blackboard in green chalk.

"Mrs McHugh!" a spotty girl with a dirty cardigan shouted from the back. "It's nous, not *nouse*. Nouse is common sense."

Beryl threw the board-duster at the girl.

McHugh threw the summons on the floor.

All the children started throwing their French books at each other.

"Anyway, it's the theatre management you've got to take the injunction out against, not me. They're the organization that is actually presenting the show. Christ Beryl, you're going too far this time."

A small boy with an angular body and thin, tragic features edged his way up to the blackboard through the confusion and wrote "shit" in red chalk, then quietly went back to his seat.

"Look love, you can have a divorce. I see what's happened to us as clearly as you do. I want your happiness, honestly I do. But don't do this to me. It's not fair. If you carry on with it I'll have to fight back."

Beryl kept her face turned from her husband and informed her class, now in turmoil, that in French one did not say "to give a cry" (donner un cri), but "to push a cry" (pousser un cri). Was that not peculiar?

"For instance, that police sergeant will testify to adultery with you. He's made a confession. He says he'll lend me a hand any time I like. And there's Lulu's observations. She's not as daft as she looks. How will that sound in the dock—an affair with an actor like Joe Woodhead?"

At the back of the classroom Georgie Thompson took his pet stoat out of his desk then released a shoe-box full of white mice.

"Go on, Ivan the Terrible!" he shouted. "Gerrum!"

Beryl, blinded with tears, wrote 'Vous poussez' on the blackboard.

Standing amid a roaring throng of third formers, McHugh launched his final appeal. As the fire-hose was uncoiled from the wall and desk-tops were torn from their hinges, he begged Beryl to come to terms. Steadfastly she refused to recognize his presence, staring out of the window as white mice were slaughtered by the merciless carnivore around her cork-heeled K shoes.

"You can go your way, I'll go mine. There's no need for us to torture each other . . ." McHugh bawled as the surge carried him into the corridor through the shattered door. "For Christ's sake Beryl, let's help each other for once instead of trying to make each other miserable. I've got to the stage with you where all I look forward to is the conflict. That's sheer sadism, or is it masochism?"

The writer was swept down the corridor by the third form. As he disappeared round the corner the headmaster entered the devastated classroom and found Mrs McHugh standing by the blackboard, butchered mice in heaps at her feet, and "Vous poussez shit" written up on the blackboard in multicoloured letters.

Pilsudski sat on God Perkins.

The rehearsal was over. It had been good. He knew that *The Blinding Light* would work, now all the new elements had been knitted into the main body of the script. Today, Fred had been co-operative. He had sat through two hours of rehearsing Act One Scene Three—absolutely immobile, his oily profile kept side on to the audience, long oily finger at the controls on the saddle horn. Somehow Fred had accepted his place. Not a walk-on. Not a spear-carrier. But a mute leading role. The way that the ex-mariner looked at it was this: *they* could see him. He was astride the most dramatic character in the cast. From under the crutch of his oily overalls bellowed the very voice of God. It would have been ungracious of any novice to expect more exposure than that on his first appearance on a public stage.

The artistic director had worked out his schedule.

It would be tight, but he could make it. Now he would go to Weldon Stack and arrange for the invitations to the opening night. All the metropolitan critics and impresarios. The whole theatre world. They would encounter in this terrible tin box with all its creaks and groans, the drumming of the rain, the draughts, the traffic noise, a dazzling image, an articulated mystery.

This catalyst would thrust deep into the subconscious of

the old-world Little Englanders and explode, driving them into more continental philosophies and dreams. It would be a talking diamond, a giant star in the grey weather.

McHugh appeared in the auditorium.

"Hello there, Ben. Just having a little vision up here. We're on to a winner with this one. I love the part where St Paul finds out his sister's pregnant by a Christian convert from Jerusalem. In fact I think that's my favourite . . ."

McHugh sat in an end-seat.

"You know we've got those two limp-wristed shitheads from the Theatrefund closeted with Sean, don't you? I've just seen Weldon. They're going to do their best to stop the play going on . . ." McHugh said bitterly. "They haven't been here for five minutes and they're taking sides."

Pilsudski grinned and patted the saddle horn.

"Leave them to me, Ben. I know all about it. Don't worry. We'll get your play on. Have you spoken to them yet?"

McHugh said that he had deliberately avoided any confrontation.

"Well, do me a favour will you? Have a word with the bastards. And I'll take you out to dinner. Come on, cheer up. We'll give that *cordon bleu* soup-kitchen up the valley a try. I fancy a bit of the old dingo vol-au-vent with some kookaburra's brains in brandy for afters. What d'you say?"


## sixteen · The Face of the Law

"Hello. Orrestwater police here. Hello."

Jules Stack sat at the switchboard taking an incoming call from a distressed lady in an outlying district who had found a group of sea-scouts raiding her raspberry-canes.

"In uniform, if you please!" She squawked. "Covered in badges!"

"Jeeeezus, that's terrible," Jules Stack sympathized. "Haven't you got a shotgun or something?"

There was a deep pause at the other end of the line.

"Is that really Orrestwater police station?" the complainant said eventually. "You don't sound like my usual man."

"Oh, they've all gone to Curdog for a conference. All the members of the Force have to be briefed on a secret operation."

"Well, who are you then?"

"I'm a stand-in."

"You're not English, are you?"

'Lady, for Chrissake, I went to Winchester and the Royal College of Music. Is that good enough for you? I may have a trace of a North American twang, but who hasn't these days? Do you listen to those pop programmes? All those witless bastards have transatlantic accents and they've never got further west than Cardiff," Jules Stack cackled throatily into the mouthpiece. "How's your raiding party? You'll have to watch those horny little mariners, lady. Once they've stripped your raspberry-canes they'll be over the window-sill stripping you. Have you got a police whistle or a can of pepper? Say, where can I get some fresh raspberries in this dump anyway? There's none in the shops . . ."

The whimpering at the other end of the telephone was clearly audible to Harriet. Leaning over the switchboard she flicked the call off.

"Hey, why the hell did you do that? I was helping that woman."

"Jules, I'd rather you went back in your cell."

"They won't be back for hours. Did you bring the cake with the bottle in it? Christ Harriet, I'm starved and my nerves aren't so hot today."

The suspended police sergeant entered the office.

"Just reporting in," he said.

Jules Stack noticed the bulges in the man's raincoat pockets and the clanking sound that he made when he walked.

"You're taking this business damn well," Jules Stack smiled encouragingly. "You don't seem to blame me at all, even though it might be considered my fault from start to finish."

"I don't bear grudges. You did me a favour. At last I know which direction to travel in. If I hadn't arrested you for trying to usurp Mr Ben McHugh's function, then I would never have realized the truth about myself. I'm a writer. You know that. You've read my stuff. I've read yours . . ."

"We're buddies!" Jules Stack laughed, his eyes fixed on the

clanking bulges in the suspended police sergeant's raincoat pockets. "Come on in. Let's talk some more. Lock us in will you, Harriet? When two artists get together they need a little privacy. Will you watch over the switchboard until the boys get back? Don't forget that the first thing to get is name and address, name and address, I can't stress that enough." Jules Stack left the desk and put an arm round his writing colleague's broad shoulders. "Come on then Mack, let's get down to business. Where I think you go wrong is in *style*, you haven't evolved a recognizable style yet . . ."

Gently he ushered the police sergeant down to the cell, Harriet following with the keys. The grizzled disciple of Mr Ben McHugh chuckled stoically.

"Give me time, mate. I'm ignorant, aren't I? I can't hope to be as good as Mr Ben McHugh overnight, can I?"

"Oh Jules, before I forget. Your brother wants you to go out to dinner tonight. Is that all right?" Harriet said, preparing to shoot the bolts.

Jules Stack pulled the cell door shut and sighed with exasperation.

"That little bastard thinks he can bribe me into forgiving him for keeping me here in the pen. If I go with him, you know what it will be? Wine with this, wine with that, brandy, liqueurs, all that shit. No sir, I'm happy here. Tell him he can stick his social life. I'm a changed man Harriet. If I can get that job, move into your flat, and we can pool our income even during my long periods of illness, then that's enough for me. You want me dried out baby, and dried out I'm going to be."

When Harriet walked back up the stairs to the office, the key ring tinkling at her thigh, she could have cried aloud with pure happiness. At last she was having an impact. She was saving a man from himself.

Behind the cell door, Jules Stack was helping the suspended police sergeant off with his raincoat, marvelling at the dense weight of two dozen cans of potent barley wine and a large bottle of Pernod.

"Now we can put this goddamned world to rights," the ex-composer said, his eyes blazing with excitement, behind his bottle-end spectacles. "By the time we've finished with human society and the body politic there'll be fuck-all left except the crumbs. And the crum-bums can have the crumbs.

What's this? Keerist, you've got a beer here, and another? No chance of sharing one with me for breakfast is there comrade?"

That evening, while sipping a flinty Manzanilla, Geoffrey Block asked for a personal transfer charge call from the Dramacart box-office telephone through to Lionel Handlegrave in London. The Moorish window was firmly closed, the door locked, and Sean stood guard with Glenda.

"What's going on?" Lulu asked from round the corner of the Thorneycroft chassis. "Why are you standing there with that look on your face?"

"Just having a breath of fresh air," Sean answered shortly. "Haven't you got some costumes to launder?"

Lulu shrugged and dodged round the side of the big lorry. Getting on her hands and knees she scuttled under the radiator, traversed the length of the vehicle, then crept across to the box-office caravan, slid under it and applied her trained ear to a crack in the floor. Her memory soaked up the conversation word for word, even capturing the subtle alterations of tone, shifts of emphasis and undercurrents of mood.

"I'm afraid that it's as bad as we expected, sir. McHugh's been struggling to superimpose a basically middle-class structure of ideals on what is a bohemian and freedom-loving organization. He's trying to destroy the old Romany spirit and replace it with materialistic values. He's an opportunist, sir . . ."

"What evidence have you got? I must have proof."

"Haven't you got the extracts from the script yet, sir?"

"What extracts?"

"Sean sent them down to you. With the testimony of McHugh's mother, the opinion of the local council, the walkouts from McHugh's current play in the repertoire, and Sean's and Glenda's evidence, I think we've got enough to stop him. *He must be stopped, sir.*"

"Tread carefully, Geoffrey. Are you certain? If we ever crush a burgeoning talent, that will be the end of us. You know our position. Our whole *raison d'être* is to encourage writers, especially new writers. Before we destroy one we must be absolutely sure of our ground. What would happen if we suppressed McHugh and then he was adopted by the Berliner Ensemble or an *avant-garde* company in Paris? We'd look the most terrible fools. You must establish beyond all doubt that he is unacceptable to the working class and that *they* see him as an élitist. Without that final proof, we have no case."

"But, sir, how can we prove that. The working class is hardly articulate about such things . . ."

"Are you saying that the working class is inarticulate?"

"No, sir, no, a thousand times no. What a thought. I'd never say such a thing . . ."

"I leave it to you and Dearden. If you cannot arrange a test of working class reaction to McHugh's work then there's not much point in your staying up there. I'll have to report along the corridor that we can't manipulate even a minor artistic situation to the national benefit. What a fool I'd look, eh? Come, come Geoffrey, don't tell me that Orrestwater is the world. Use your head. Resolve the issue . . ."

"Yes, sir."

"And don't involve me. All I want to hear is either that you've abandoned the whole wretched provincial business, or you've brought it to a successful conclusion. If you are discovered to be at the centre of any shinnanicking or devious Machiavellian backstairs politicking then I will disclaim any knowledge of you, or your mission. This conversation is at an end. Good luck, Geoffrey."

"They said Ben McHugh was destroying the old Roman spirit," Lulu whispered to Weldon Stack as the front-of-house manager teased his hair with a suede-brush. "Do you know what that is, Weldon?"

Weldon Stack put on his dinner-jacket and fluffed out the wings of his maroon velvet bow-tie.

"The Romans were very well organized. I can see what they mean if they reckon that Ben jeopardizes our efficiencies. But that's not the point. What is important is whether Ben has any talent. Do you think he has any talent?"

"He's got a talent for upsetting people. Did you hear what he did to Beryl? He went down to the school and caused a rumpus. She's been fired. Oh, she's very unhappy now. Poor Beryl. I feel very sorry for her."

Lulu brushed Weldon Stack's shoulders free of dandruff and checked him over for general sartorial presentation.

"They also said that what mattered was the working

class. If the working class don't like Ben McHugh then he's for it. Would you say that Beryl was working class?"

"Of course. She's obsessed with money. What could be more working class than that? But I think the Theatrefund see things differently . . . is my collar straight? . . . you see, they're obsessed with *class*."

"You've got class, Weldon. I think you're smashing."

"Thanks, Lulu. Do you like my cuff-links?"

"I wish I could come to swish dinners with you. Don't forget to make sketches for me of all the dresses that the women are wearing. You look very dashing Weldon. You suit evening dress. Why don't you love me?"

"Chemistry, Lulu, chemistry. I'll bring you back something."

"Christ almighty, Weldon," Lulu sobbed, "I love you so much."

"Lulu, don't . . ." Weldon Stack sighed. "You know we've been through all this before. I'm fond of you but . . ."

"Fond? What's fond? I worship you. Don't bring me cheese and biscuits like last time. I'll be waiting for you."

Weldon Stack chucked Lulu under the chin and ushered her out of his caravan. His mind was already on the alert, forecasting the nature of the social and political interactions that would take place around the millionaire's dinner-table that night. He was glad that Jules had cried off from the engagement. Tonight Weldon Stack would have to give all his attention to the business of selecting his position in the forthcoming battle for power. From what Lulu had told him he could estimate the type of weaponry that would be used and the fundamental issues at stake.

Sean made some swift calculations, looking round the table.

In the glow of seven electro-plated silver candlesticks sat the source of an audience. Geoffrey Block had spent a morose evening, toying with his food, refusing to charm his host and hostess. Now Sean had the means of cheering him up. Was this the time to pounce? The dinner party had reached the liqueur stage and most of them were volubly drunk, their conversations sliding off the subject into genial laughter and banter. Sean would not have an opportunity like this again. His hands tightened under the table. Would they listen to him? Was it worth risking Weldon Stack's support? He had not yet committed himself to the management cause. With the drama officers at his back he could insist that the front-of-house manager keep his mouth shut about the test audience, claiming that it was an official experiment for the Theatrefund. Weldon Stack was still working his way through a piece of Blue Wensleydale and a large glass of port, regaling the lady councillor with stories about his rowing days at Oxford. Now was the time to strike. Make it light-hearted. Disguise the serious intent beneath a surface of glowing wit. Sean launched himself into his idea, drawing the attention of all.

"Everyone here has been generous to the Dramacart, given it their help and support over the years. We have always wanted to find a way of showing our appreciation but what we can do is limited—usually it means complimentary tickets. After all, that's the only currency we have. What we would like to do this year is a little different. Would you all think it a good idea if we invited all your workfolk to a performance? There's the council labourers—the dustmen, street-cleaners and such. There's your staff on the island, Ed —you must have fifty people in the kitchens and gardens— all the other businesses which are represented here. I calculate that we could make up a full house . . ."

Geoffrey Block stirred, interest brightening in his tired eyes.

"I think that sounds rather fun," the chief executive of Orrestwater said from behind a gigantic Havana cigar, "We could lay on some sandwiches, free beer, yes, I like it . . ."

"Do you envisage this as a kind of charity night?" Ed asked from the head of the table, his small, slight figure lost in a huge carved chair. "I would be prepared to chip in, say five pounds to cover the ice-cream in the interval. How much are the programmes now?"

Sean thanked his friend effusively, then folded his hands together. From the expression on his high-domed features, grim, heavy, suddenly serious, a man wrestling with a great problem of conscience, the dinner guests could see that the initial phase of the discussion was now past. Sean had more to say. More to ask of them.

"I would like all your working people to come and see *The Unfathomable Grass* next Friday," he said gravely.

There was a shocked silence. The lady councillor dabbed nervously at her mouth with her napkin.

"I can't send my riding instructors to see that filth!" she protested eventually. "They'll all go off the rails. Can't they come and see something else?"

Geoffrey Block smiled across the table and drew his chair closer. If there was a moment in his career when he must confide in The People, then it was now. He must trust to their good judgement and basic common sense. With these leaders of the working class by his side he could confound McHugh and all the forces of the *nouveau riche*. Gently, with fine skill and charm, he prised the masterly plot of Sean Kel out into the open, a miner exposing a reef of pure gold. At the end of the exposition there was a deep, satisfied silence. The chief executive was smiling. Glenda was beaming pinkly. Dearden Ryan was twinkling. Sean was the only sombre guest, gazing across the table at his cause for thought: the unknown quantity.

Weldon Stack.

"You'll fix this all up then, Weldon?" Sean asked as casually as he could. "Tickets at the box-office. Free bar. Everything to go like clockwork. No hassles. I'd like to give them all every opportunity to enjoy the play. It should be an interesting evening. I'll inform Peter. Leave that to me. No need to advertise it otherwise we'll get all the Women's Institutes and Gardening Clubs asking for hand-outs. Do I make myself clear?"

Weldon Stack nodded. Sean noticed, with some pleasure, that his front-of-house manager seemed to be regarding him with frank admiration.

## seventeen · McHugh versus McHugh

Beryl heaved her bicycle into the back of the estate car owned by the spiritually derelict sports master whom she had collected on her final exit from the staff room. The bewildered retired rugby crackerjack, a nervous apprehension successfully hidden beneath a drooping moustache, stood by the driver's door, eyeing McHugh. He wore knitted yellow gloves.

"Why are you going off with this deadbeat?" McHugh asked concernedly. "Couldn't you wait until someone more suitable turned up?"

"Bob's worth ten of you! His feet are on the ground!" Beryl screamed as she hurled hundreds of copies of *Good Housekeeping* on top of the bicycle. "He'll take care of me. Won't you, Bob?"

Bob nodded diffidently, pulling up the imitation fur collar of his imitation leather motoring jacket.

"I don't want any trouble," he stated flatly. "We can be grown-up about this whole thing. All we need is fair play."

McHugh shook his head with impatience. He knew Bob. The faded champion of track and field was a notorious local character, haunter of alebenches, fund of endless tales from a brainlessly physical past. McHugh himself had been jumped on from dark corners by Bob and bored daft with his stories. For Beryl to live with him was an unimaginable slight on McHugh's manhood. To prefer that kind of idiotic tedium to the adventure of theatre! McHugh spoke of his reservations.

"Beside a man like Bob you're nothing," Beryl retorted savagely, her arms full of dresses still on coat-hangers. "He towers over you. If you had half his common sense and charm you'd be a lucky man. Here's the key to the caravan. I hope it burns down with you and all your manuscripts in it. Bob and I are going to find a new life together, and I'm going to be happy for once!"

Beryl slammed the rear door of the estate car, her pale face pink with exertion and rage. McHugh stepped forward to open the passenger door for her. Beryl lashed out with a tall glass figure of a Siamese cat and smashed it over McHugh's head.

"Now see what you've done!" she wailed. "Mum gave us that. Christ, Ben, I hate you. Bob, hit him for me! Hit him! Before we go! Please, Bob, hit him! Do what you showed me in the assembly hall, that flying kick to the throat! Come on darling . . . for me . . ."

Bob crept out of the driving seat and looked at McHugh across the bonnet of the car.

"You've treated her badly," he mumbled through his moustache.

"Bob, I wouldn't have bought you so many pints if I'd

known what you were going to do to Beryl. Let her go. Don't exploit her present need. She's had a rough time. I know that as well as anyone, and now she needs a real friend. Bob, I know you once took eight perfect catches in the slips to defeat the Giggleswick second eleven for less than double figures, but this time be less sharp-eyed and agile. Don't catch my wife on the rebound. Can't you just piss off for a while, go on a refereeing course or something?"

McHugh's pleading only antagonized Beryl's saviour. Placing one sinewy hand on the bonnet of the estate car, Bob vaulted athletically across and landed in front of McHugh in a ferocious pose, hands held stiffly in front of him like twin cleavers, legs bowed and braced.

Beryl clapped her hands from the front seat of the vehicle and threw open the door, screaming encouragement.

"In the throat darling! Hit him in the throat!"

Bob's small brown eyes shrank into pinpoints. His moustache quivered. Rising on the balls of his chukka boots he launched himself into a lethal, gravity-defying flying drop-kick. McHugh flung himself to the ground, allowing the ageing footboxer to soar over his head and make a horizontal entry into the passenger side of the estate car where Beryl was still exhorting her new lover to destroy the old. They collided with a grinding of bones, sighs and whimpers.

Sean stepped out of the box-office, his mind locked on to the working-class audience that was due to visit the Drama-cart that night. Behind him, Glenda was stamping tickets. When he saw a slouched and dishevelled McHugh, heavy with the cares of the world, sliding into the driving seat of a strange estate car and driving off with two bodies tangled in the passenger seat, he immediately rang the local police station. Even McHugh could not get away with murder.

> Oh the Mounties always get their man,
> The Mounties catch their fellow,
> The Eskimos don't stand a chance,
> And Redskins are plain yellow.

Sean took the receiver away from his ear. Behind the two ebullient male voices at the other end of the line he could hear a clanking sound. He was confused.

"Haven't heard that for a long time," Weldon Stack reflected as he pencilled in the seating plan. "Went down very well at the Ottawa Arts Centre in 1964. It was the first opera that he ever attempted—and, I stress, there was no conscious imitation of *Rose Marie*. Not bad for a first effort in that genre. In fact I think *The Berserk Bear Trapper* did quite good business. Do you want the sewage attendants in the back? They will change before coming I hope. Any ideas about the employees from the chinchilla farm?"

McHugh did not drive far. When he saw that Beryl and her deliverer were coming round he parked the car and got out. He watched while Beryl tended to Bob, stroking his head, clucking and crooning. McHugh found himself moved by the scene. Beryl had never consoled him. She had never taken him in her arms to comfort him. Why? What did Bob have that McHugh did not have? Why had Beryl fought him for so long? Here she was, tired out, desperate, clinging hold of her only salvation. Beryl needed someone, but it could never be McHugh. She had often said that all McHugh needed was himself. This was untrue, but Beryl was blind to her husband's needs and the basic verities of his personality. What he needed was *help*. Actual, physical, real *help*. Support. To share. To give and be given in return. A deep twinning of his soul with someone else's. Another half.

Slowly Beryl unravelled herself from the shattered athlete and stroked his damaged pride. She was as tender as a mother with a child. Emotion rose in McHugh's throat. Perhaps Bob was the answer to Beryl's prayer. He was going nowhere, which was Beryl's goal. She wanted peace, and peace was anywhere but the site of McHugh.

Breaking cover, the writer walked round to the open window.

"Do you want me to make you an allowance?" he said in a low, careful voice. "I suppose I should, now you're unemployed."

"We want nothing off you!" Beryl replied, Bob's head held to her breast. "We'll stand on our own two feet. Just leave us alone."

"I'm sorry, Beg . . ."

"Don't call me Beg, you bastard."

"If you promise not to carry on trying to get my play prosecuted under the Theatre Act, I'll keep away, give you grounds for the divorce, anything reasonable. All right?"

Beryl stared into the driving-mirror, appalled at the way her mouth refused to stop trembling.

"Please, Ben . . . go away. I never want to see you again."

"Aren't you going to wish me luck?"

Beryl shook her head.

"Not even a farewell kiss?"

Beryl turned her face away. Bob opened his eyes, looking straight into the face of his erstwhile target. He struggled to get into a sitting position but Beryl held him close.

"Bob, you heap of parasitic sporting history," McHugh hissed into the dazed ear of the declining champion, "I feel very guilty about leaving Beryl with you, but as it seems to be what she wants, I've got no choice. Try and improve will you, for my sake? Find a new self." McHugh paused, looking at his wife. "Good-bye."

McHugh turned away and walked along the road back to Borrans Field. A moment later Beryl drove the estate-car up on to the pavement in a last bid for revenge, knocked McHugh into a wall and sped away laughing.

McHugh lay by the wall for several minutes. He was not seriously hurt but he kept still in case the impact had broken bones or inflicted an internal injury. Carefully, he spat on to the pavement and studied the saliva for blood. This could be the end. Numb with shock, aghast at the full extent of Beryl's hatred, he was incapable of returning to any real feeling about himself. His wife had tried to kill him. He had managed to turn a human soul against him to that cruel point where his death had been sought after: Beryl had wanted him out of the world, out of circulation, out of the way. Warily, he coughed and spat again. No blood. He stirred his legs, nerves bunched up against the anticipated agony. Was there any blood coming from his ears? His nostrils? With slow care he explored every outlet of his body.

"Hey, are you okay?"

McHugh took his hand out of his trousers and glanced upwards. A tall, serene, smiling woman in a long brown flowered dress and a maroon shawl, daisies in her long black hair and a large raffia bag in her hand, was looking down at him with warm concern in her crinkled, hazel eyes.

"Why did those people try to run you down? Have you double-crossed the *Cosa Nostra* or something?"

McHugh noticed the American accent, the companionable, direct, easy approach of the woman as she sat down next to him and opened her raffia bag.

"Do you like picnics? We were at the caves yesterday. Have you been there? I can never remember whether it's the stalagmites that go up or the stalactites that go down. Do you like tuna? Wow, feel that sun. Ah, this is great. See that butterfly. We found a plant in the caves. Can you believe that? Only artificial light. There it was, on the edge of a pool. Only about an inch, but trying. A lesser stitchwort the guide said. Here's to the lesser stitchwort. Want to share my picnic? There's enough for two. For three. I eat too much. Mmmm, that sun is so warm. Greek brandy is more expensive here. Do they put the prices up for the tourists? See, you're not so pale now you've had a drink. Have some more. Those are Missouri biscuits. Yes, you look a lot better. I guess they only winged you. Who was it? Sorry, I won't pry. Do you know, I'm the slowest driver ever to go on the freeway? That's what this traffic-cop said. Isn't it great to sit here and watch the world go by? I've never been here before. Everything is so accessible. Never climbed a mountain in my life. Have a pear. Go on, have that big juicy one. I guess you might be able to help me. I'm looking for this crazy theatre. I hear there's a great show on at the moment, something about grass. Some friends of mine saw it and they said it was very good and they're so critical . . ."

McHugh saw the sun radiating from behind her head as if she wore a halo of golden blazing light.

He heard the soft talk; friendliness, generosity, warmth flowing from her as the lazy stretches of a river in a summer of endless sun.

With a grateful sigh, neglecting to find out who she was, where she came from, or whether she was available, he fell hopelessly in love.

Harriet drove past McHugh and Bonnie Lou, for such was her name, without affording them much attention. Uppermost in her mind was Jules Stack's interview in two hours time over at the Freshwater Research Laboratory. In order to get the ex-composer across the lake and in spick and span condition to meet the Chief Biologist she needed to have the writ of habeas corpus presently held by Weldon Stack. When she arrived at the theatre she found the front-of-house manager engrossed in conversation with Pilsudski and only with difficulty could she wheedle him away for a moment. Weldon Stack agreed to the release of his brother with few regrets. He had no wish to jeopardize any opportunity to get the ex-composer into a settled job with an income of his own. Harriet drove back to the police station and served the writ on Jules Stack and the suspended police sergeant who were seated at the switchboard singing "Valencia" to a hot-dog stall owner whose means of livelihood had caught fire and was requesting assistance. Before they left the station the telephone lines were switched through to Curdog and the cell was tidied up. Harriet hung the keys on the hook, straightened a framed warning against giving false information, and closed the door. An hour later, Jules Stack, having had a bath and his trousers having been sponged and pressed, appeared before the Chief Biologist, Harriet at his side while the suspended police sergeant watched baby trout in a glass tank in the main hallway.

"Do you think that you can handle delicate glass instruments?" the Chief Biologist asked, remembering the piano at the Normality party.

"I've been handling delicate glass instruments all my goddamned life!" Jules Stack chuckled. "I'm a natural for the job. Show me the way. How much sick leave do you get here?"

The Chief Biologist informed the applicant that the staff got sick leave when and if they were sick.

"Yeh, but how much? A month? Two months? What about during a bronchial winter? Ever had hay fever? Is there a canteen? Do they vary the menu? What about outings? In Canada a lot of my buddies used to get a Christmas bonus and a sabbatical every four years. Do I get a sabbatical?"

"Mr Stack, the job that you are being interviewed for is not all that high powered. It is for a Helper Grade Three in the roe-seminalization section. Impressed though I am with your education and background, I don't see us being able to draw on it for the functions you will have to undertake . . ."

"I'll sort him out," Harriet whispered hurriedly. "He's a

little confused. Don't worry. Leave him to me. He'll be on time every morning and he'll be a credit to the lab. Won't you Jules?"

"Too damn right I will. Will I get an office like this?"

The Chief Biologist sat back in his chair. He knew that he was taking a chance. Harriet was a well-trusted and efficient employee. In the past he had allowed himself to delegate too much authority to his junior staff. There were times when he wondered who was running the laboratory, he or Harriet?

Now he knew. All doubt cleared from his mind.

It was Harriet. She had him securely by the balls.

One weekend in Barrow-in-Furness and here he sat, power-less. Signing the employment documents he placed Jules Stack, for the first time in a long and colourful career, firmly in the ranks of the working class.

That evening the invited audience was pre-assembled in the Orrestwater Drill Hall to receive instructions from their chief executive. All Ed's gardeners were present, the pockets of their old corduroy jackets crammed with corrupted organic matter. Beside them sat the kitchen staff, various offal and left-overs carried in plastic carrier-bags. The lady councillor's riding instructors bore large polythene sacks of horse-manure and even the assistants from her gift shops had chipped earthenware rabbits modelled on Beatrix Potter characters stuffed into their handbags. The dustbin-men had been allowed to select their own means of expression and sat in a bunch, some with their fingers looped through the handles of old suitcases and Gladstone bags, others holding objects under their coats. One street-cleaner had a dead cat wrapped in newspaper across his lap while his friend, an Asiatic, with a livid scar across one cheek, dangled four pairs of muddied baby's reins and a clutch of used condoms from his ungloved hand. Labourers from local farms had brought sacks of turkey-droppings. Men from the local brewery sat about with hold-alls full of used malt and cracked wooden bungs. At the back stood four ladies from the tourist office with missiles made up from last season's brochures tied together with string and elastic bands, soaked in paraffin.

"Well, what have our friends from the Freshwater Research Laboratory brought?" shouted the lady councillor, noticing that the sturdy working folk from across the lake seemed to be led by a strange hound-faced man with a silver-topped walking stick whom she did not know.

"What the goddamned hell did you expect us to bring? Fish of course!"

Jules Stack opened up his jacket to reveal transparent envelopes hung on a string around his neck. Inside the containers circled baby trout, perch, tench, roach and the rare char which is only found in certain waters of the Lake District. The ex-composer shook the envelopes to disturb the fish.

"Show them what we've got, lads!" Jules Stack commanded, turning to his contingent. "Don't you worry, lady. We'll do our bit. Christ, my first day at work and I get an outing! How can I help but be enthusiastic?"

When the Freshwater Research Laboratory group had settled down amongst the rest of the working-class audience, the Council tea-ladies distributed the first of a series of handouts. Jules Stack was gratified to find himself being pressed to free beer and sandwiches.

"Jeeezus, I should have done an honest job a long time ago," he said to the suspended police sergeant who had tagged along. "No wonder there's so many people in employment. They've got it made. Grab me another beer before she goes away will you? What have you got in your sandwich? Do you think they've got any pickle? One thing you northerners do well is pickles . . ."

The chief executive got to his feet and began the briefing.


## eighteen · Test Run

Weldon Stack was already off-balance and feeling that he was in the centre of an uncontrollable situation when McHugh appeared at the entrance of the foyer with Bonnie Lou smiling on his arm. Two minutes earlier Weldon had confronted his elder brother, strangely rotund, at the head of a sub-group of the working-class audience which had arrived for their free performance at the Dramacart. In answer to Weldon's natural questioning of his elder brother's presence in such a gathering, the jovial ex-composer had merely chuckled and nudged a close companion, an untidy, grizzled chap whom Weldon had recognized as the police sergeant active in the arrest and incarceration of Jules Stack. The front-of-house manager could not add all this up. The sum was impossible. He squinted sideways at McHugh and waved his great bush of hair, then tried to close the door.

"Not tonight, Ben. We're full up . . ."

McHugh put his shoulder down and kept the door open.

"Weldon, what the hell are you playing at? It's me, Ben! I've got a right to see my own work . . ."

Bonnie Lou peered through the opening of the half-shut door.

"This is the right place isn't it, honey?"

Weldon Stack shoved harder and tried to connect the bolts. McHugh gave a grunt of frustration and burst through, knocking the front-of-house manager against the display board which carried photographic portraits of the cast.

"We're booked out!" Weldon Stack insisted. "Please, Ben . . ."

"Don't give me that. I know you always have house seats put by . . . Christ, Weldon, this place stinks," McHugh frowned as he led Bonnie Lou towards the auditorium entrance. "Why don't you get it properly cleaned? We'll just slip in at the back."

"Ben, every seat is taken. Don't make trouble, not tonight. Sean and Glenda are in there with the drama officers . . ."

"That's unusual isn't it? A full house? I'll get a few quid at nine per cent of a full house."

Weldon Stack made his last stand, blocking the entrance doors. He did not appear convinced that he had much chance of preventing McHugh and his new woman from seeing the play. But it was his duty to try. With a huge false smile he spread his arms and waited for the inevitable punch.

"Get out of the way, Weldon."

"No, Ben. You have no right to cause a disturbance. Come tomorrow."

"There's no performance tomorrow. We're going to do this élitist coterie performance of *Dream* on this *nouveau riche* shithead's island . . ."

"Come on Monday."

"Bonnie Lou goes back to London on Sunday. This is her only chance to see it."

"Lend her a script."

"Hon, I can always come back another time . . ."

"Look love, I haven't seen my play yet. We're going to see it together and we're going to see it tonight! Now get your arse out of the way, Weldon, or, friend or no friend, I'll lose my temper and create the kind of trouble that might occur in your worst FOH nightmares."

"Ben, I'm begging you now . . ."

"Weldon, who's been the one preaching to me about my responsibilities? You. Who told me that I had a *duty* to see my own play? You. You're my moral guide for Christ's sake. And now you're trying to stop me facing up to myself. Weldon, try to understand. I can go in there and watch tonight because I have someone with me who *understands*. She'll help me, from within. Now come on, open that door. You should be glad that I'm coming to terms with myself."

"It's a charity performance," Weldon Stack said with sudden cruelty. "They haven't paid."

"That bastard Sean giving away my money again," McHugh snarled, heaving the front-of-house manager to one side and barging through, dragging Bonnie Lou behind him. "It doesn't come out of his salary, I notice!"

Inside the auditorium the house-lights were still up. McHugh saw that Weldon Stack had been telling the truth. Every seat was taken. This struck him with less force than the stench which hung over the audience.

"Say, is there something dead in here?" Bonnie Lou asked.

"I'm sorry, love. This old heap of scrap-iron is on its last legs. God knows what's stuck under the floor. We'll have to stand up at the back." McHugh whispered, putting an arm round Bonnie Lou's waist and holding her to him as he leant against the back wall. "Don't forget. All I want is honest criticism. Tell me exactly what you think."

The audience murmured excitedly as the house-lights dimmed.

The curtains slowly parted.

McHugh groaned, left Bonnie Lou's side and went into the foyer where Weldon Stack was checking a fire-extinguisher.

"Can't this fucking company get anything right, Weldon? They've got the wrong set up," McHugh hissed.

"You insisted on going in, Ben," Weldon Stack replied evenly, blowing down the black rubber tube. "Don't blame me."

McHugh went back into the auditorium. As he did so,

Murphy Winspear entered from stage right in a silver lurex costume and black velvet cloak.

"Oh Christ," McHugh seethed into Bonnie Lou's ear, "even the costumes! Even the costumes! What a balls-up!"

A confused murmur rose from the row where the general manager, assistant manager and the drama officers were sitting.

> Now, fair Hippolyta, our nuptial hour
> Draws on apace; four happy days bring in
> Another moon: but, oh, methinks, how slow
> This old moon wanes! she lingers my desires
> Like to a step-dame, or a dowager,
> Long withering out a young man's revenue.

Murphy Winspear held centre-stage, his eyes narrowed, peering out into the darkness, his fine declamatory baritone shaking with tension. He could hear the buzz of wonderment. Pilsudski had warned them that this audience might be volatile. He had asked the cast to be careful tonight, on their toes.

"Plagiarist!" came a cackling accusation from the middle of Freshwater Research Laboratory block. "We've heard that before!"

"That doesn't sound like Mr Ben McHugh's style at all," said a voice which had once contained Authority. "Perhaps it's ironical?"

"Do we start throwing things now?" asked a gruff, agricultural person in row B. "Is it now, or must we hold on?"

Joan Earth swept on in a long filmy lilac dress that was split down to her navel. On her dark head rested a glittering crown. Members of the male audience who had been ready to cast the first missile quietened down and sat back in their seats while she floated over the boards, her naked feet shining in deep blue footlights. The opening of many handbag clasps smote the air and the grinding of female teeth.

> Four days will quickly steep themselves in nights;
> Four nights will quickly dream away the time;
> And then the moon, like to a silver bow
> New bent in Heaven, shall behold the night
> Of our solemnities.

A deep, sexual sigh heaved up from the corduroy trousers and overalls of the working-class audience as Joan Earth stopped moving her lovely mouth. There was a pause, profound, stirred, highly charged.

Murphy Winspear, more confidence in his stance, threw out an arm in a broad dramatic sweep.

> Go, Philostrate . . .
> Stir up the Athenian youth to merriments;
> Awake . . .

Murphy was not permitted to finish his speech. A sullen murmur filled the auditorium, mixed with exclamations of anger. The actor stepped back, flinching.

"Go fill your what?"

"Go fill your stratly?"

"Bloody old fairy in drag insulting us! Who does he think he is?"

"Do we start now? Is that the signal?"

"Hon, why have you approached your subject so obliquely? Is this going to be some kinda cultural collage?"

"Sean, what's going on here?"

"Keeeerist, what a fink! He's lifted the opening straight from . . ."

The dead cat sailed through the gloom and wrapped itself around Murphy Winspear's neck like a bolas. He screamed, choked and fell to his knees. Joan Earth bent over to help him and received the full brunt of a barrage from the gift-shop assistants, hundreds of chipped earthenware rabbits raining down on her splendid haunches. In the next salvo came the envelopes of fish which burst, scattering their contents all over the stage where they wriggled and flashed in the strong lights. Large plastic sacks of horse manure burst with tremendous force while cracked wooden bungs rattled against the scenery. Tripes, lights, bloody viscera and the testicles of neutered cattle wrapped themselves around the standing lamps and batteries of overhead illumination, drenching the deep blue footlights with grease. From backstage came Pilsudski, waving his arms about and leading on the rest of the cast. Huddling together they took all the punishment that the working-class audience could hand out, now led by Jules Stack who was standing on his seat urging them on, bellowing war-cries and singing snatches from his adaptation of the death-chant of Huron warriors.

Finally Bert rang down the curtain, but not until the audience had expended itself. The air was thick with passion, the reek enormous. Behind the curtain Pilsudski embraced his cast one by one, checked them for injuries, then hared round to the front of the theatre where a crowd of local pressmen had gathered on the promise of news from an anonymous caller several hours earlier. With the working-class audience pouring past him, rosy with pleasure, chattering, laughing, the artistic director told the story of the assault on William Shakespeare by the people of Orrestwater.

"Now can you see the problem of taking theatre to theatre-less areas? Where else in the world would you find people behaving like this? They never gave the old Bard a chance. I should think the poor old bastard is spinning in his grave right now. But we won't give up. This experience has taught us something. What the people round here want is new plays, not something that's three hundred and fifty years old. The past is the past. We take this as a demonstration of support for new writers, new plays, the future. We forgive them . . . you hear that? We forgive you!"

A great cheer went up from the dispersing crowd.

The journalists scribbled away and the man from the local radio station pushed his microphone nearer.

McHugh sat in the foyer, speechless with admiration for Pilsudski's ploy. Bonnie Lou held his hand, a frown on her face, thinking his silence was a symptom of nervous hysteria or shock. She tried to comfort him.

"Hon, I've seen action theatre off-Broadway. I've seen Liquid Theatre. I've seen Anti-Theatre, Non-Theatre, but this is way out. All that *feeling*, and so spontaneous. I heard that you English were so controlled and socially repressed..." Bonnie Lou hugged McHugh closer. "Thanks for bringing me. If this is what happens when you do Shakespeare, I can't wait to see a really controversial play . . ."

Sean, Glenda and the drama officers waited until Pilsudski had finished giving his press conference before interrupting. They were tight-lipped, pale and indignant.

"That's it, Peter," Sean said, his voice quivering. "You've alienated the Dramacart from its support. We can never come here again. You've gone too far this time. We're finished . . ."

As if to underpin the general manager's analysis of the massive emotional upsurge that had taken place in the Dramacart that evening, the police then arrived, accompanied by several ambulances and a fire-engine. Householders living nearby had heard the tremendous noise coming from the theatre and had phoned the police station. As the lines had been switched through to Curdog by the ex-prisoner and the suspended police sergeant, it had taken time for the anti-riot team to get themselves out of the secret operations briefing and into their vehicles.

The general manager and the artistic director were asked to explain what had happened to the heavily armed superintendent after the white-haired officer had stripped off his gas-mask.

"We're used to a quiet life up here. Better you take this bloody contraption elsewhere if this is the kind of thing that's going to happen. We've had our eye on you for some time . . ."

"Come off it, sport. It was the restive Poms who started it. Would you throw horse-shit at Shakespeare? A cultured man like yourself? I bet you went to a good school and learnt to love the old *Midsummer Night's Dream* . . ."

The superintendent was astonished to discover the true facts.

"They broke up a performance of *Shakespeare*? Not that obscene stuff you've been showing here? Oh dear, that's different. You hear that, lads? What a thing to do. Where are they? We can knock them off. Fancy our theatre-going public behaving with such disrespect. The magistrates will be hard on them, by God we'll show them. Up the hill, lads. We can round most of the buggers up . . ."

Pilsudski pleaded with the superintendent.

"No, don't take it out on them. In some ways that audience was only trying to move you Poms and your outdated thinking into the second half of the twentieth century. We've forgiven them. Can't you do the same?"

The superintendent was silent for a while. He could hear the working-class audience shouting and laughing on its way home, on the ferry over the lake, in the terraced houses by the quarry and down the wide streets of the council estates. It had been a long time since the superintendent had heard such signs of life this late on a summer's eve. His heart softened.

"All right. But you'll have to move on. I want you out of here by Sunday night. I can't risk any more trouble than what I've got on my plate right now. We've got a panic on at the moment. There's some top men coming up from London tomorrow for a big purge of some kind. God knows what it is, but I have to have every man on stand-by. Take note then. Out of here by Sunday."

"What about next year?" Sean asked, his burning eyes fixed on Pilsudski. "Will we be welcome next year?"

"Lad, who can see that far ahead? Next year is next year. It's the future. Anything could happen. We live in changing times."

The anti-riot squad re-boarded their vehicles and drove away. Pilsudski was left with Sean, Glenda and the drama officers. Further down the foyer sat McHugh and Bonnie Lou. McHugh was smiling, his eyes never leaving the animated features of his Australian hero.

"You've done it then, Peter," Dearden Ryan drawled, hooding his eyes to make them cool and sardonic. "You've effectively destroyed the Dramacart. No other council will ever let it into their district now. The one subsidized theatre that had true integrity—once—is rendered useless. By your machinations you have not only brought down the theatre itself, but also the livelihoods of your actors, and even the writing career of the man you claim to believe in. Tonight you helped the Dramacart to commit suicide."

Pilsudski appeared sombre, thoughtful.

"You may be right, Dearden. But we'll leave this area with something to remember us by. Sean, I know I've been precipitate, but I want you to know that I won't let you down tomorrow. All right, tonight we made a mistake—but have a heart, Sean, playing in repertoire isn't easy, trying to remember what show comes on what night. I think the company do a good job keeping track. How would you like a change of identity each night, and playing two or three parts at the same time? It's a schizophrenic freak-out! Who are they for Christ's sake? Where's their personal character? Sunk without trace when they work for this theatre. We expect too much of them. But tomorrow, tomorrow is another day. We'll give you a performance on that island that will go down in the folk-memory of these rustic Poms, Time immemorial won't be in it! We'll go out with a bang.

Christ, Sean, I owe you that much. Come on, shake. Shake my hand. Let's make up and be friends like the old days when you first asked me up as guest director for *Journey's End*. Remember that opening night Sean? Remember? You stood here, tears in your eyes, and you hugged me, you sentimental old bastard. Wasn't your old dad knocked off by the Krauts on the Somme? Or was it Ypres? No matter. Let that old comradeship live again. We'll work together. We'll have them rolling in the herbaceous borders tomorrow. What better setting for *A Midsummer Night's Dream* than a midsummer night on a dream island? I believe he's got a terrific pad out there. Towers and battlements, griffins in the garden, fountains. Sounds bloody beautiful to a man raised in the outback. And then, Sean, we'll find another corner of this country to take the old battle-wagon to. Why not Cornwall? Or the Hebrides? America? We don't have to limit ourselves to this part of the land of the Poms. The world is our oyster, Sean, we can go anywhere we want. They'll welcome us with open arms. That's better, see, now you're smiling again. Christ, Sean, how long is it since we've smiled at each other? Doesn't that feel better? Now we're in business again. Together. Side by side we'll lick the old Poms, knock down all their old tabus, re-fire their boilers, get them on the move again. Wahey! Christ, we can win again. We can do it!"

Pilsudski pulled a stunned, twitching, bewildered Sean Kel into his arms and bussed the general manager on both cheeks, then strode through the entrance doors into the auditorium. Bert was swabbing the stage with a mop and bucket, his nose wrinkled.

"I'm leaving," he muttered. "This is the last time that you and Weldon talk me into anything. Make a fookin change you said, give 'em what they're not expecting. Look at my fookin stage! It'll take all fookin night. Why can't you do some Gilbert and Sullivan instead of this fookin intellectual rubbish? I'm fair fookin worn out. Look at those dirty braces on my hair-driers. There's a fookin French letter jammed in the tape-recorder as well. I want my cards . . ."

Pilsudski patted the stage-manager on the shoulder, an up-curving simian grin on his broad chin.

"Come off it, Bert. Theatre's in your blood."

"And every other bugger's by the look of it," Bert sniffed,

unwrapping several yards of pig's intestine from the stage-right mask of tragedy which adorned the wall.

## nineteen · Island of Dreams

Weldon Stack sat in his caravan with the general manager and assistant manager. There was a curious hardness in his slavonic eyes and the knife with which he buttered a piece of French bread prior to discharging a full can of anchovies on to it, was steady and unflurried in its operation. At his right hand a coffee percolator bubbled and steamed, interspersing the steely address that the front-of-house manager was making to his superiors.

"Call a board meeting by all means, Sean. By the time the Dinky Toy Division have got here, pumped up the tyres, played choo-choos with the Thorneycroft and diagnosed the fault in the fuel pump on the Bedford, I'll have had time to give them the full background to yesterday's abortive *coup de théâtre*, including a detailed statement from someone who was actually at the briefing given by the chief executive of the Orrestwater Council, plus a sworn statement from an officer of the Law who was also there . . . do you appreciate your position? Do you want Dearden and Geoffrey placed in the position of being seen to have actually *conspired against* the development of new drama? Will they thank you for that? You may find the publicity offensive—but who rigged the initial stages of the demonstration? If that had been Ben's play . . . well, I suspect you would have been all smiles this morning. Then there's always the matter of your sexual nepotism isn't there? We've had the *News Of The World* on the phone this morning. All I'd have to do is drop a word in the right quarter. It isn't worth your while. If you'll take my advice just try to forget the whole issue . . ."

Here Sean laughed hollowly and ground his worry beads together.

"You treacherous beast, Weldon!" Glenda shouted, red in the face.

"Treacherous? To what?" Weldon asked levelly. "One has to balance things out. What one must always consider is the main principle. That, in this case, is the *ideal* of theatre. Who supports that here? Who are its defenders? Who risks most for it? I'm afraid, without wanting to be unpleasant, that I can only pass a private judgement on your relationship with the ideal. You are both leeches on it. You make it neither stronger nor brighter. You feed off it from the bottom end, like some rather befuddled parasites on the roots of a tree. Will you go away now? You are putting me off my breakfast."

Sean shot up from his seat and his sinewy artisan's hands reached out for Weldon Stack's Afro hair. In his mind was a murderous thought which involved holding the front-of-house manager against the wall while Glenda poured boiling coffee in the porches of his ear.

Weldon Stack blocked Sean's attack and locked fingers with the furious theatre executive, staring meanly into his bloodshot eyes. Alarm spread over Sean's face as the front-of-house manager slowly forced him to his knees, exerting a wristy strength once used as the stroke in his college boat.

"Sean," Weldon Stack said coldly, "in the theatre you cannot win. It is not even the winning that matters, but how you lose. Your way is the worst I have ever encountered. You should leave the theatre and administer a pension fund, or sell double-glazing."

Glenda helped Sean to his feet, her round moon face drained silver, a circle of pure hatred. Her plump country-girl's body trembled, her sheaf of blonded hair swished through the air as she lugged the sobbing general manager down the steps into the sunlight.

"It's mine!" Sean moaned. "It's mine! The Dramacart is mine!"

Glenda gazed into the cool, slavonic eyes of Weldon Stack, two shafts of steel shooting from her crimson wrathfulness.

"We gave you a chance, Weldon, we trusted you. Not any more though. Now we know where you stand. You'll be crushed along with Pilsudski and McHugh. We will win, in the end. We will. We're not cynical. The Dramacart belongs to those who believe in it, not those who use it."

Glenda paused, her red mouth working like a glove puppet. Weldon Stack kept his eyes steady, boring past the dark gun-sights that the assistant manager had trained on him from her pupils, past her fury, past her hatred, seeking the *principle*. Glenda flinched momentarily, then responded strongly.

"I wouldn't care if we went round with an aquarium in it, or an exhibition of silver snuff-boxes, the important thing is that *we should keep going round*! That's the real ideal!"

Weldon Stack nodded, a little smile lifting the corners of his thin lips. He was satisfied with that answer. It represented the cause of the parting of the ways, gave justice to both sides, and was, after all, Glenda's peculiar expression of truth.

Somehow it salved his philosophical soul.

Ed, the millionaire, had hired two launches to be used in transporting the Dramacart company and all their theatrical paraphernalia from the jetty at Orrestwater across to the island. Towards five o'clock Bert drove the juddering Bedford down to the launches and unloaded crates, boxes and hampers and the costume skips. The company, it being another gloriously sunny afternoon, chose to stroll down from Borrans Field in their own time. When they arrived at the jetty they were surprised at the amount of attention that they received from photographers and numerous sad-faced men smelling of drink who wanted their life-stories. On the benches along the marina sat more reserved characters, most of them clutching hard-backed copies of books about *La Nouvelle Vague* in contemporary British theatre and the drama of social force and interaction.

Hampstead had become a ghost town.

The Fleet Street haunts of the journalistic guard-dogs of the nation's cultural standards were deserted.

All day long the trains, motorways and sky-roads from London to the north-west had been full of poetasters, writers manqués, academic gravy-train professors in the underground theatre of the 1940 Blitz, reviewers who, for the first time since the General Strike, had rushed from their lunchtime comforts to leave the capital, jaded critics, trend-setting publishers, all the twisted yarns in the massive, cosy over-coat of British culture were in Orrestwater, waiting for trans-port to the island. Patient, hopeful, kept warm by frequent trots up to the off-licence and meeting so many old friends, they hummed and gossiped, glancing at their watches, sending their keen, far-seeing eyesights over the shining lake to the mysterious island where the tall trees sheltered an explosive secret—that performance of *Dream* that had actually penetrated the absorbent, indifferent, spongy consciousness of the working class.

Further along the lake shore, hidden from public view by a copse of tall ash trees, Fred was laying out a jetty of his own with oil-drums and planks. At the end of the makeshift harbour rode a raft made of large timber balks. Aided by Pilsudski and McHugh, Fred finished the job and walked back to the Dramacart. When they arrived there McHugh found, to his dismay, that Jules Stack and his friend, the suspended police sergeant, had been spying on them.

"Look man, we just wanted to talk to you about how much stage-direction to put in this play we're writing . . ." Jules Stack explained. "We didn't mean to pry. Jeeezus, we don't even know what you're up to. Let us in on the secret. We're on your side. When we discovered that last night had been a deliberate attempt to sabotage your career, we came straight down to give our support."

"That's right, Mr Ben McHugh. When Mr Weldon Stack told us the truth, well, we were bitterly ashamed to have been part of such an underhand business," the suspended police sergeant said in affirmation. "What can we do to help?"

Before Pilsudski could think of a way of getting rid of the two would-be writers, Fred rode God Perkins out of the scene-dock. He stopped the mechanical horse by Pilsudski and McHugh who then threw a canvas groundsheet over Fred's head. There was a hole cut through for the rider and the coarse fabric settled down over the throbbing quadruped, touching the ground on either side and effectively hiding it from sight.

"Mother, what a stroke of . . ."Jules Stack spluttered through the fumes, "Ben, you've got an imagination that outpaces Mark Twain and Lewis Carroll put together."

"We've got to walk it on to the raft," Pilsudski explained. "If you want to help, go on ahead and check if anyone is around. It mustn't be seen."

Fred put God Perkins into first gear and slowly rode it

away from the Dramacart, through the trees and on to the shore.

Sean and Glenda had a long heart-to-heart conversation in their purple caravan after their discussion of ethical principles with Weldon Stack. They decided that it was still worth trying to keep the Dramacart going, hoping that Pilsudski and McHugh would move on to the new theatre by the time that the next season started. There was the problem of the increasing cynicism of Dearden Ryan and Geoffrey Block who were both still in the toils of profound depressions as a result of seeing horse-shit hurled at Shakespeare, but Glenda thought that she had enough pull in the metropolis to recoup their losses and establish a new situation. If the performance of *Dream* worked, if they could extend the audience to the whole middle-class theatre-going public of the town, there was a chance of re-creating goodwill towards the Dramacart, enough for an invitation to return next year—without Pilsudski or McHugh—and put the travelling theatre on its proper footing. Glenda telephoned Ed and explained their thinking to him. He agreed to their idea of inviting as many serious theatre patrons as possible, mentioning the fact that he had been plagued all day by people swimming ashore at his island and hiding in his rhododendrons until his eight Irish wolfhounds were suffering from nervous exhaustion and overwork.

"They all say that it's the play they've come for. I had a chap here at half past eight this morning wearing a skin-diving suit, says he's from some magazine or other. From what I understand the idea of putting *A Midsummer Night's Dream* on in these idyllic surroundings is attracting world-wide attention. They've taken quite a few pictures of me with my dogs and even a few of the staff. You know, Sean, I have a feeling that we should capitalize on the situation and get as many influential people over here tonight as possible. Throw your net as wide as you like."

Lionel Handlegrave tried to comfort his drama officers who were lying in their twin bedroom at a four-star hotel, their breakfasts untouched on a silver tray between them, eyes fixed on the ceiling.

"I've never been so ashamed of being human," Dearden

Ryan whispered. "God, what humiliation. I hate the majority. Sir, you can discharge me from service for saying that, I know, but it was a truly horrible experience."

Lionel Handlegrave nodded thoughtfully, lighting a long thin Cuban cigar.

"Difficult to imagine."

"Thank you for coming up so promptly, sir," Geoffrey Block whimpered pathetically. "We thought you should see for yourself. I couldn't go through that again, sir. They just shouted Him down, sir, throwing their sweaty nightcaps in the air. They're repulsive, sir!" He screamed suddenly, his head leaving the pillow. "They're hideous, deformed, unfeeling!"

"Is the production all that bad?" Lionel Handlegrave asked gently, patting Geoffrey Block on the shoulder as the drama officer slumped back into a prone position. "I mean, even *He* can be done badly."

"No, sir, it's quite good, I mean the girl was quite lovely . . ."

"Why did they do it then?"

"They couldn't tell the difference, sir. Can you credit that? They couldn't tell the difference between the poison of that *nouveau riche* pornographer McHugh and the most delightful, sylvan, joyous, frothy comedy written in the English language. Is it worth going on sir? I wonder. I really wonder . . ."

Dearden Ryan heaved himself up on one elbow, shaking his head, frank despair in his haunted eyes.

"Don't make me go again tonight, sir. I couldn't bear it."

Lionel Handlegrave pushed out his lower lip and looked stern.

"Duty, Dearden, duty. We'll have to see this thing through to the end now. The die is cast. We're up against it. Pilsudski and McHugh are somehow promoting a radical revision of well-tried cultural values through their subversive activities. I don't know how they're doing it but I intend to find out. Try to sleep now."

Geoffrey Block groaned.

"I'll have nightmares, sir, I know I will."

Lionel Handlegrave looked at his watch and drew on his cigar.

128

"An hour to go, and then we'll have to get aboard. Get some rest men. We could have a hard night ahead of us."

"But Harriet, I honestly didn't expect him to be off sick on his first full day here. Surely that's unreasonable. It doesn't seem right to me . . ." the Chief Biologist said with as much good nature as he could muster. "Also I think it's a bit thick when he rings in to inquire about his sickness benefit thirty minutes after he was due to start work. It makes me suspicious."

"He can't help it if he's not well," Harriet said fiercely. "Don't you ever give people a chance? Poor Jules has had a difficult life, his constitution is not strong, and he's got a lot of problems. All you want to do is put him in a position where he'll see life as hopeless. He'll probably commit suicide. I know him. He's a sensitive person. If you continue to persecute him I'll report you to the Labour Officer, the union, and your wife."

The Chief Biologist watched Harriet storm out of his office.

Was he really interested in Freshwater Research any longer?

Did he want to stay with his wife?

Did anything matter?

These thoughts ploughed through his tired mind as he tried to return to a pile of laboratory reports on the temperature environments best suited for the development of salmon hatcheries. Looking up for a moment he saw the island of the millionaire resting on the silver plain of the lake. If only the Chief Biologist could cut himself off from the world like that, surrounded by spawning fish, the centre of teeming ocean life. On the shore would be his wife, Harriet, Jules Stack, the rest of Mankind. The Chief Biologist would be fertile only unto himself.

With a sigh he returned to the neat data compiled for his eye. Tonight he would continue this dream, while watching a pastoral enactment of another vision, a vision wrought from the riches of an equally worldly-wise soul.

Fred gingerly rode God Perkins on to the ramshackle jetty, testing the strength of the planks. Step by step he edged the mechanical horse along. As he slowly made his way out to the raft, Weldon Stack appeared, leading a small shaggy hill-pony by a length of rope, keeping his distance so that the muddy hooves of the animal would not dirty his green suede boots.

"Christ, Weldon, I wanted a horse, not a dwarf!" Pilsudski shouted back from his place waist-deep in the lake, helping to support God Perkins along the planks.

"This is all I could get. It seems very amenable to discipline," Weldon Stack called out over the quiet murmur of God Perkins. "Surely it will do. After all, it is a kind of horse, not so?"

Fred guided God Perkins on to the raft. McHugh and the suspended police sergeant, now up to their necks in the lake, held the floating platform steady until God Perkins could be got to the centre. Then Weldon Stack led the biddable hill-pony along the jetty and tethered it close to God Perkins.

"All aboard!" Jules Stack cried from his hiding-place among the trees. "All clear! Wait for me! Keeerist, what an experience. Here let me give you a hand boys."

Jules Stack helped McHugh, Pilsudski and the suspended police sergeant out of the lake.

The raft strained at the holding rope.

Fred inserted a long pole into a socket, turned up a cross-piece and unfurled a large canvas sail, then handed out beech saplings to the crew.

"We're going to need some effort off you non-technical lads now. Get along each side, search for the bottom. Keep together now. Will you cast off, Weldon? That's right, undo the knot. Come on lad, weren't you ever in the Scouts? Here we go. Where's the wind? By God, this takes me back to when I was on the Kon-Tiki. Here we go! All together now!"

The raft moved away, the canvas sail filled.

The hill-pony snickered and rubbed his soft muzzle against the hidden head of his *doppelgänger*.

Only Dunkirk could have rivalled the scene as hundreds of little boats, coracles, yachts, steamers, power-boats, skiffs, dinghys and pedalloes headed for the island as the summer evening settled into a warm, tranquil light and the birds around the lake shore began their quieter songs. Anything which floated and could bear the weight of a man was on the lake's surface. The shingle shores were devoid of craft.

Old vessels, long disused, were afloat, their crews steadily baling out. Moored yachts, owned by weekend sailors from Manchester and Liverpool, were stealthily boarded, their anchors raised, and sailed away. Even the ferry, normally held between two stout hawsers and plying in a predetermined voyage from side to side, was hijacked and the skipper forced (though he was not unwilling after fifteen years on his route) to head for the island.

Through this motley flotilla, unnoticed and arousing little comment, sailed the raft bearing God Perkins and his living counterpart, poled along by pioneers of the living word.

## twenty · World Première

"Sean, isn't it marvellous!" Glenda breathed, surveying the throng. "We can win! I feel it . . ." She stopped dead, staring through the crowd. "It is! She's here! Look! Oh this is fabulous! We can introduce her to Lionel, he can get her story first-hand!"

Glenda pointed across the front lawn of the towered eighteenth-century folly which was Ed's home. Through the crowd Sean could see an old lady sitting on a granite sphere held between a squatting dragon's half-open wings. As they started to cross towards her, Ed pushed his way through the jostling multitude, anxiety written over his swarthy countenance.

"Sean, there are literally thousands of people here. They're in every room in the house. There are men from London asleep on all the beds, others in the kitchen trying to force the padlocks on the fridges, the breakages are enormous. There's one odd chap trying to prise open the cellar door with a silver-topped cane and every time I try to stop him his friend, who seems to be a very disreputable person, threatens to arrest me. We've just caught two ice-cream salesmen, plus all their wretched equipment, landing on the north shore. The dogs wouldn't even try. They've given up. They're defeated. I'm beginning to feel that I can't call my home my own . . ."

Sean took Ed aside, man to man.

"Ed, you want to be known as a patron of the arts. Tonight is your big chance. The New Year's Honours list is not far away from this very spot right now. We can make a breakthrough. Look at them! Every critic in London is here. For the first time in twenty years, the Dramacart is getting into the national Sundays. And why? Because of your generosity. Don't lose your nerve. Stick with us. Trust us. Your name will be in every paper that matters, we'll see you receive all due recognition."

Glenda wandered purposefully across to where Mrs McHugh was smoking a contemplative cigarette.

"How nice to see you again," Glenda smiled, sitting down on the flat tip of the dragon's left wing. "Have you come down from Carlisle?"

"Oh, hello dear. What a night-out this is. Such a crowd! There's no other play could get me out of the house on a summer's night you know, especially when there's all those thermostats in the cellars to watch and millions of those bloody spores. Oh, you've no idea how hard I have to work with those things. I've brought a few basketfuls down to try and flog in the interval if that's all right with the organizers. Do you think they'll mind?"

Mrs McHugh lifted an edge of her long grandma-style dress and revealed a large basket full of mushrooms.

Glenda forced a cheerful smile to mount the rosy hills of her cheeks.

"I don't think they'll object. It looks as though you won't be the only one selling things . . ."

Glenda nodded to a man in a white coat pedalling a tricycle and white refrigerated box of ice-cream amongst the crowd, ringing his bell, followed by eight exhausted Irish wolfhounds.

"All the world and his wife are here," Mrs McHugh twinkled with enjoyment. "I'm really looking forward to this."

"Don't go away will you? I'll see to it that you get a good seat. After the show I'd like you to meet some people. I must rush now, there's so much to do . . ."

Glenda gave Mrs McHugh a smile, a squeeze of the hand, then shouldered her way back through the crowd to where Ed was still in conversation with Sean, his sharp bird-like head bent forward, pecking at Sean's good reasons for letting the situation ride. The general manager had reached the point where Ed was kneeling to receive his knighthood at the hands of the Queen.

"Ed, it is men of commerce who must be the new patrons of the arts. Who can replace the Earl of Southampton?"

Jules Stack, with the aid of a dozen drunken hacks who had been gathered from the billiards-room, eventually managed to charge down the door of the cellar. Within minutes the word had been passed round the entire journalistic contingent that the cocktail party had at last started and free drinks, their natural perquisite at all such functions, were to be had. A human chain was made down the steep stone steps and all Ed's wines were passed up from their resting-places, finding new homes in the pockets of crumpled jackets and soiled raincoats. To one side of the ex-composer stood the suspended police sergeant who put one bottle aside for every two passed up into the hands of the thirsty newshounds.

"Do you see any snacks down there?" a rich metropolitan voice boomed down the stone steps. "Any canapés or devils-on-horseback? We're starving. The bloody kitchen staff have locked themselves in and won't open the door. Strange lot these provincials. We haven't got long before this play starts on the lawn. God, even a sandwich would do."

"Nothing like that down here," Jules called back, glancing down each vaulted chamber. "Hey, wait a minute. What's this? Yeh, there's some carcasses here boys. Mmm, smells all right. Meat. Meat all right?"

"Too bloody right! Pass it along!" bellowed the choleric critic who was suffering from pangs of hunger. "I could eat a bloody horse."

Jules chuckled as he unhooked the hung sides of decomposing venison and passed them up, the vision of God Perkins and the hill-pony uppermost in his mind as the incongruous duo had paced through the trees from the shore, guarded by a circle of watchful men. Jules Stack would have liked to see the press corps getting their dentures sunk into a slice of God Perkins. From upstairs he heard the sound of tearing flesh and loud exclamations of approval.

"Now for a feast of something entirely different," Jules Stack said to his friend, clapping him on the shoulder. "Let us go up and see the birth of a new age."

"Right, Mr Jules, out of here, out of the smell of age and decay, cobwebs, history, the immutable past, out into the brightness of a morning . . ." the police sergeant breathed as they mounted the steps. "To the future, Mr Jules!"

"Come on, man, keep it coming!" The ex-composer chuckled. "You're definitely developing a style of your own."

The audience began to settle themselves down on the lawns below the imposing façade of the house. They were in holiday mood and the press corps spread their growing bonhomie through the theatre-goers with all the liberality of those giving away that which never belonged to them.

The giant personality slowly calmed, quietened, began to anticipate the start of the play.

Their eyes turned from each other to the empty half-circle of sward lying beneath the dark, upraised towers.

From his position by the bole of a birch tree, Peter Pilsudski gave the nod to Bert. The show was now in his capable hands.

The floodlights on the folly dimmed.

Lamps strung from branches were brought up to full power.

A full, expectant silence fell on the crowd.

Glenda sought Sean's hand and held it tight.

Sean closed his eyes. The waiting was unbearable. Now it was all or nothing.

From the depths of a yew bush came the clip-clop of horses.

"Ask Cecil if I can have a bit of his Nuits St George if I give him a swig of my Armagnac . . ."

"Is there marrow in the bones of deer? Do you think they'd have a marrow-spoon here?"

"Hush!" hissed the crowd. "Hush! Hush!"

"Sean . . ." Glenda quavered. "He's changed the opening."

"Honestly Nigel, it's Château Lafite, and a good year . . ."

A platoon of Roman auxiliary soldiers burst out of the trees in pursuit of Joan Earth. Brazen trumpets bellowed over the loudspeakers. The Early Christian virgin was pounced on and tied to a tree. From stage right entered Bert with a wheelbarrow crammed with instruments of torture. He dumped it beneath the spread-eagled lovely and shuffled off, back to the lighting board.

134

The audience buzzed, intrigued and excited.

A visiting university professor from the Massachusetts Institute of Technology edged forward with a tape-recorder, a Japanese model of phenomenal cost, and lay full length at the front of the acting area, a microphone held thrust out in his hand. His face had the radiance of discovery.

Paul of Tarsus entered on the hill-pony.

The auxiliaries lit a small fire of twigs, then sprang to attention while one of their number held the silver bridle of the hill-pony for Joe Woodhead to dismount.

Glenda hammered at her chest with her fists, driving the evidential gemstone hung round her neck deep into her pure country-bred flesh, needing the pain, wanting to confess the guilt which had lain behind her futile hope.

"Give her the sign of the fish!" Paul of Tarsus commanded.

"I am ready to suffer for my faith," the Christian-cracker's long-lost sister said bravely.

"Do your worst. Don't I know you from somewhere?"

"Not that I remember."

"You have a look of my father. He was a Greek psychopath like yourself."

While the branding iron was heated in the fire, Joe Woodhead stood below the Early Christian virgin, stripped off her robe, produced a pointer from his saddle-bag (chased in gold with the sign of the eagle), and addressed the overwhelmed audience.

"This," he said, tapping Joan Earth's skull with the tip of the pointer, "is the cavern in the poison sea, the submarine cathedral of evil, the house of the creeping horror which will rise to devour the world . . ."

The lady councillor walked out.

So angry was the female politician that she strode into the darkness, through the trees, right round the island, then reappeared stage right just as Joe Woodhead had reached the mammary glands in his anatomical dissertation on the threat of the Early Christian movement.

The enthralled audience watched the pointer toy with the magnificent bosom of the bound neophyte.

"Rubbish!" the lady councillor cried, marching across the acting area and into the darkness again.

"Oh that counterpointing is brilliant!" murmured the reviewer from *Time Out*. "See the way he takes the eye in two directions, suggesting the basic Pauline dichotomy of spirit. Out of sight."

"The navel of this cruel, senseless faith!" Joe Woodhead intoned, prodding the spot on the smooth unblemished belly of the tree-borne beauty. "The push-button of the infernal Christian computer. The womb-trigger! The feed-lock for re-fuelling in flight of the faithful from their stratofortress father in heaven! What soft secrets lie behind this peep-hole? Will we see the leering face of the Christian Lord in the convolutions of these sacrificial entrails? Will he dare to occupy the body of his worshipper, or has he fled to his high places, his tail between his legs? At the approach of an empire based on Reason, does not the alleged emperor of Love have a responsibility to stay and argue the toss? In the agony of his adherents, should not this King of Life take action to relieve them with something other than death?"

Hordes of lesser critics cast covert glances at the grand masters of their art, the men from the *Sunday Times* and the *Observer*, trying to interpret their expressions. Were they with this adventurous new work, or against it?"

Both men had their eyes riveted on the pointer.

Their jaws hung slack against their deep-winged lilac shirts and butterfly bow-ties.

Their features exposed an absolute involvement in the fate of the Early Christian virgin. They cared. They were moved. As the pointer traced a wavering line downwards they both leaned forward in their collapsible chairs, fascinated, hypnotized.

The view of the critical body swung to the affirmative and constructive.

As the pointer descended, two Early Christian revolutionaries swung down from the trees on vines, sten-guns on their hips. In a cacophony of crackling gunfire, the Roman auxiliaries retreated, Paul of Tarsus at their head. Joan Earth was cut down from the tree.

Pause. A grinding of gears.

The Early Christian revolutionaries and Joan Earth sank to their knees.

Through the massive trunks of beech, oak and elm, came a flashing figure, a whirring, prancing apparition ridden by a dark-skinned, aloof man.

Enter God Perkins.

136

"Get dressed!" boomed the great voice from under the saddle horn. "Cover thy nakedness! Remember Eve in Eden! The glory of God, which is thy glory O child of Nature, is only for the eyes of the Saved!"

God Perkins did his controlled rear.

Fred, sombre, stiff, dignified, sat his mount, in his expression a deep intelligent satisfaction. All eyes were on the mechanical horse. They were not even bothering to watch Joan Earth get dressed. That machine was the focus of attention. Fred could feel the waves of sheer awe radiating from the great crowd.

"Who is the true God, the master or servant?" God Perkins bellowed.

"Oh the servant, master!" the two revolutionaries and Joan Earth chanted.

"Who is the true Power, the horse or the rider?"

"Oh the horse, the horse!"

God Perkins did two controlled rears and batted his stiff tail from side to side.

Fred rode his master along the front fringe of the audience, putting God Perkins through his paces, using little grace steps which he had devised after seeing six white circus horses from Vienna on a television programme. At the end of the equestrian display the audience broke into spontaneous applause. God Perkins bowed his fearsome head and cantered back to his three waiting worshippers, great hinged mouth synchronized with the roaring saddle.

"The way through to this Heathen Heart is through his mount. Let it be known among our people that the hirsute steed of this Paul of Tarsus, the sturdy bearer of his terrible pride, shall be secretly known as Mount Sinai from this day on. We will work from below, and from above. We will crack this nut. We will sunder his shell. Away!"

The three Early Christians kissed the raised metal hoof of God Perkins then trotted back through the trees.

"Christ, Ben, I like that adaptation for the hill-pony. Your mind works so *fast*," Pilsudski whispered. "Do you think *shaggy* might have been better than *hirsute*?"

McHugh closed his eyes, nerves tingling, mind racing.

It was *working*!

Pilsudski's voice was thousands of miles away.

All he was conscious of was the massive electric bond

between his words, his images, and that giant personality camped beneath the towers. The only human contact that was small and yet within his management was Bonnie Lou's hand, clasped in his.

The men from MI5, Army Intelligence and the County Constabulary looked across to the island, saw the changing lights and heard the baying of a great concourse. Behind them were four hundred fully equipped men. The mission to track down the secret weapon rumoured to have been clandestinely developed in the scene-dock of a travelling theatre, and actually sighted by an ex-employee of Naval Anti-Espionage, was now in full swing.

"Sir, there are no boats left. Everything is already being used. Even the British Rail steamers."

"The activists are obviously having a bloody convention over there," said a tired, sophisticated major-general who was eyeing the lighted advertisement over a nearby saloon bar. "Let's get them when they come back. They can't stay over there indefinitely, can they?"

"Can't do that. We must break it up. Call in the helicopters."

"We haven't got any helicopters."

"Then get some."

"Sir, the nearest choppers are in County Durham."

"Then get through to them, now—now!"

"I suppose the men could swim, sir."

"Of course the men can swim. What do we have all this combat training for if the men can't swim? In fact, if I remember correctly, one of their tests is to swim five miles in full kit plus rifle and ammo. It's only a mile or so to that damned island. Get them into the water."

"Will you be joining us, sir?"

"You know I'd love to but, well, it's eardrums. Can't get water in the old eardrums. Meningitis. Get them down to the water's edge then. We've got no time to waste. I'll hop over with the helicopters. Good luck."

Slowly four hundred heavily burdened men were herded down to the shore and, under the appreciative eyes of tourists taking an evening stroll along the marina, driven into the lake with harsh words of command and prods from the swagger-sticks of enthusiastic officers.

At the interval all the journalists headed for the telephone, fighting with each other to ring their precipitate reviews, desperately trying to meet Sunday deadlines. No form was observed, even the most venerated critics had to take their place in the tumultuous and inspired queue. While they waited, the metropolitan newsmen swapped mouthfuls of vintage wine, exchanged wildly enthusiastic comments on the play and vied with each other in the construction of telling phrases which could be photographed, enlarged and stuck up outside theatres in St Martin's Lane and Shaftesbury Avenue.

"Bravely brilliant!"

"Dazzles the mind with dithyrambic dialectic dissonance!"

"Cuts through the fat of contemporary acquisitive society to the very bone of human existence!"

"The fusion of the Industrial Age with the Age of Despair! A new prophet of the Inanimate! The death of the Christo-Marx Culture! Hampstead Man Devolves! The Exponent of Metallic Nihilism! This will run and run and run!"

Jovial laughter and applause greeted these sallies, contrasting with the embittered gloom of Sean and Glenda who were waiting to telephone for a berth on the ferry from Stranraer to Ulster, anywhere to get away, anywhere.

"Look at them!" Sean said through clenched teeth. "Look at those bastards, all over Pilsudski. They couldn't give a damn whether McHugh was *nouveau riche* or the commandant at Auschwitz."

Sean glared along the corridor to where Lionel Handlegrave, Dearden Ryan and Geoffrey Block were congratulating the artistic director on the first half of the performance.

"He's not going to get away with it!" Glenda shrieked suddenly, spying Mrs McHugh passing with her basket of mushrooms crying 'Nice and fresh! All hand-raised!'

Glenda seized Mrs McHugh by the elbow and steered her to the assembled drama executives, interrupting the stream of phrase and praise.

"Now tell them what you told me about your son, Mrs McHugh, please, it's very important!" Glenda said with a shaking voice. "They should know what he's really like. Tell them what he did to you, about his background."

Mrs McHugh set down her basket and folded her arms.

"About our Ben? You want me to tell these people about

what a bad bugger our Ben has been? The way he joined the Workers Action Committee on the docks when he was fourteen and fought on the barricades in Lime Street when they wanted to close down The Vines public house? I'll tell 'em, God I will, and gladly. What a life we had with him me and his Dad. He'd never go to the Young Conservative Club dances or help with the regatta. When we bought him a sports car he just set fire to it and pushed it down the causeway into the Mersey . . ."

Glenda staggered back, blanched, speechless.

Pilsudski put an arm round Mrs McHugh's shoulders.

"Ben gave you a bad time then Ma, but he's a good writer isn't he? You must be proud of him now, eh? Things have changed."

" 'Course I'm proud of him. What we've seen here tonight speaks up for all of us doesn't it? It's about the whole human condition. Our Ben leaves no one out. He's for everyone, our common plight. Where is my lad? I feel like giving him a big kiss."

Mrs McHugh turned away. Pilsudski excused himself and followed her, carrying the basket of mushrooms. When he had caught up with the old lady he slipped the worn handle into her hand and whispered into her ear.

"Thanks Sonia. You've convinced me that you can do the old girl in *Arsenic and Old Lace*, you know the one I mean, the gentler one. You can count on that for the first season in the new theatre. Don't accept any other bookings for September/November love. Thanks again."

A voice over the amplifiers announced that *The Blinding Light* would recommence in three minutes' time.


Face to face.

Paul of Tarsus stared grimly into the eyes of Fred atop God Perkins.

The crucial confrontation.

Up in a mountain ash tree, Bert stood poised with a pan of magnesium powder and an electric switch.

The Early Christians and the Roman auxiliaries swung back and forth in a weird eurhythmic chant.

> *Will Man and Machine*
> *Explore the unseen?*

*Will Motor and Heart*
*To Infinity dart?*

Bert fired the magnesium flare. A brilliant light hit the heavens. From the shores of the island came a hoarse, exhausted chorus of cries as four hundred men in sodden clothing and equipment picked themselves up off the shingle and made a stumbling charge towards the explosion by which Paul of Tarsus was to become a Christian saint, evangelist and hero.

Through the rapturous clapping of the audience, now on its feet, staggered the saturated professionals, guns at the ready.

Four helicopters hovered over the island, their searchlights sweeping the towers and trees. The occupants bawled at the wildly cheering audience through electric bullhorns, advising surrender. As the roaring machines descended on the lawn they cast a great wind which blew the long dresses of the idle rich into shining streamers and swept the lawns free of ice-cream papers and programmes for an unwitnessed performance of a classic fantasy. In the pandemonium of this ultimate confrontation between Authority and Art, the writer, McHugh, slipped away to his future.

Taking a rowing boat from the shore he helped Bonnie Lou into the rudder seat and gave her the steering-strings. Then he pushed off, fitted the oars into the rowlocks and navigated his way through the fleet of assorted craft anchored around the island.

Soon he was away from the clutter, out in open water. The blades of his oars dipped slowly and rhythmically into the lake.

"Where are we going, hon?" Bonnie Lou asked softly.

McHugh did not reply, but pulled away from the island with its noise and confusion, heading for the peace of the tranquil lake, the quiet of the rising summer moon, and the pleasure of a hard-won, unguessed victory.

The island would not disappear.

He was only leaving it for a while.

"Hon, are we headed any place?"

McHugh raised one oar out of the water and rowed the boat round in a large circle, making two jinks with crossed blades, then straightened out on to his original course straight away from the island.

"What are you doing, hon?"

McHugh sank his head on to his chest and heaved on the oars. The boat surged forward, a musical babble springing up under the bow. He rowed until he could row no more, then rested his tired arms on the oars.

Bonnie Lou looked at him, then over his shoulder.

She smiled, understanding.

For McHugh had written on the lake.

An A which was already melting into an arrow and then into the B of a beginning.